BALZAC AND THE LITTLE CHINESE SEAMSTRESS

Born in China in 1954, Dai Sijie is a filmmaker who was himself 're-educated' between 1971 and 1974. He left China in 1984 for France, where he still lives and works.

Dai Sijie

BALZAC AND THE LITTLE CHINESE SEAMSTRESS

TRANSLATED BY
Ina Rilke

VINTAGE

Published by Vintage 2002

4 6 8 10 9 7 5 3

First published in Great Britain by
Chatto & Windus 2001

Vintage
Random House, 20 Vauxhall Bridge Road,
London SW1V 2SA

Random House Australia (Pty) Limited
20 Alfred Street, Milsons Point, Sydney
New South Wales 2061, Australia

Random House New Zealand Limited
18 Poland Road, Glenfield,
Auckland 10, New Zealand

Random House (Pty) Limited
Endulini, 5A Jubilee Road, Parktown 2193,
South Africa

The Random House Group Limited Reg. No. 954009
www.randomhouse.co.uk

A CIP catalogue record for this book
is available from the British Library

ISBN 0 09 928643 2

Papers used by Random House are natural, recyclable
products made from wood grown in sustainable forests.
The manufacturing processes conform to the environ-
mental regulations of the country of origin

Printed and bound in Great Britain by
Cox & Wyman Limited, Reading, Berkshire

PART I

THE VILLAGE headman, a man of about fifty, sat cross-legged in the centre of the room, close to the coals burning in a hearth that was hollowed out of the floor; he was inspecting my violin. Among the possessions brought to this mountain village by the two 'city youths' – which was how they saw Luo and me – it was the sole item that exuded an air of foreignness, of civilisation, and therefore aroused suspicion.

One of the peasants came forward with an oil lamp to facilitate identification of the strange object. The headman held the violin upright and peered into the black interior of the body, like an officious customs officer searching for drugs. I noticed three blood spots in his left eye, one large and two small, all the same shade of bright red.

Raising the violin to eye level, he shook it, as though convinced something would drop out of the sound-holes. His investigation was so enthusiastic I was afraid the strings would break.

Just about everyone in the village had come to the house on stilts way up on the mountain to witness the arrival of the city youths. Men, women and children swarmed inside the cramped room, clung to the windows, jostled each other by the door. When nothing fell out of my violin, the headman held his nose over the sound-holes and sniffed long and hard. Several long, bristly hairs protruding from his left nostril vibrated gently.

Still no clues.

He ran his calloused fingertips over one string, then another . . . The strange resonance froze the crowd, as if the sound had won some sort of respect.

'It's a toy,' said the headman solemnly.

This verdict left us speechless. Luo and I exchanged furtive, anxious glances. Things were not looking good.

One peasant took the 'toy' from the headman's hands, drummed with his fists on its back, then passed it to the next man. For a while my violin circulated through the crowd and we — two frail, skinny, exhausted and risible city youths — were ignored. We had been tramping across the mountains all day, and our clothes, faces and hair were streaked with mud. We looked like pathetic little reaction-ary soldiers from a propaganda film after their capture by a horde of Communist farm workers.

'A stupid toy,' a woman commented hoarsely.

'No,' the village headman corrected her, 'a bourgeois toy.'

I felt chilled to the bone despite the fire blazing in the centre of the room.

'A toy from the city,' the headman continued, 'go on, burn it!'

His command galvanised the crowd. Everyone started talking at once, shouting and reaching out to grab the toy for the privilege of throwing it on the coals.

'Comrade, it's a musical instrument,' Luo said as

4

casually as he could, 'and my friend here's a fine musician. Truly.'

The headman called for the violin and looked it over once more. Then he held it out to me.

'Fogive me, comrade,' I said, embarrassed, 'but I'm not that good.'

I saw Luo giving me a surreptitious wink. Puzzled, I took my violin and set about tuning it.

'What you are about to hear, comrade, is a Mozart sonata,' Luo announced, as coolly as before.

I was dumbfounded. Had he gone mad? All music by Mozart or indeed by any other Western composer had been banned years ago. In my sodden shoes my feet turned to ice. I shivered as the cold tightened its grip on me.

'What's a sonata?' the headman asked warily.

'I don't know,' I faltered. 'It's Western.'

'Is it a song?'

'More or less,' I replied evasively.

At that instant the glint of the vigilant Communist reappeared in the headman's eyes, and his voice turned hostile.

'What's the name of this song of yours?'

'Well, it's like a song, but actually it's a sonata.'

'I'm asking you what it's called!' he snapped, fixing me with his gaze.

Again I was alarmed by the three spots of blood in his left eye.

'*Mozart. . .*' I muttered.

'*Mozart* what?'

'*Mozart is Thinking of Chairman Mao*,' Luo broke in.

The audacity! But it worked: as if he had heard something miraculous, the headman's menacing look softened. He crinkled up his eyes in a wide, beatific smile.

5

'Mozart thinks of Mao all the time,' he said.

'Indeed, all the time,' agreed Luo.

As soon as I had tightened my bow there was a burst of applause, but I was still nervous. However, as I ran my swollen fingers over the strings, Mozart's phrases came flooding back to me like so many faithful friends. The peasants' faces, so grim a moment before, softened under the influence of Mozart's limpid music like parched earth under a shower, and then, in the dancing light of the oil lamp, they blurred into one.

I played for some time. Luo lit a cigarette and smoked quietly, like a man.

This was our first taste of re-education. Luo was eighteen years old, I was seventeen.

A few words about re-education: towards the end of 1968, the Great Helmsman of China's Revolution, Chairman Mao, launched a campaign that would leave the country profoundly altered. The universities were closed and all the 'young intellectuals', meaning boys and girls who had graduated from high school, were sent to the countryside to be 're-educated by the poor peasants'. (Some years later this unprecedented idea inspired another revolutionary leader in Asia, Cambodian this time, to undertake an even more ambitious and radical plan: he banished the entire population of the capital, old and young alike, 'to the countryside'.)

The real reason behind Mao Zedong's decision was unclear. Was it a ploy to get rid of the Red Guards, who were slipping out of his grasp? Or was it the fantasy of a great revolutionary dreamer, wishing to create a new generation? No one ever discovered his true motive. At the time, Luo and I often discussed it in secret, like a pair of conspirators. We decided that it all came down to Mao's hatred of intellectuals.

We were not the first guinea pigs to be used in this grand human experiment, nor would we be the last. It was in early 1971 that we arrived at that village in a lost corner of the mountains, and that I played the violin for the headman. Compared with others we were not too badly off. Millions of young people had gone before us, and millions would follow. But there was a certain irony about our situation, as neither Luo nor I were high school graduates. We had not enjoyed the privilege of studying at an institution for advanced education. When we were sent off to the mountains as young intellectuals we had only had the statutory three years of lower middle school.

It was hard to see how the two of us could possibly qualify as intellectuals, given that the knowledge we had acquired at middle school was precisely nil. Between the ages of twelve and fourteen we had been obliged to wait for the Cultural Revolution to calm down before the school reopened. And when we were finally able to enrol we were in for a bitter disappointment: mathematics had been scrapped from the curriculum, as had physics and chemistry. From then on our lessons were restricted to the basics of industry and agriculture. Decorating the cover of our textbooks would be a picture of a worker with arms as thick as Sylvester Stallone's, wearing a cap and brandishing a huge hammer. Flanking him would be a peasant woman, or rather a Communist in the guise of a peasant woman, wearing a red headscarf (according to the vulgar joke that circulated among us school kids she had tied a sanitary towel round her head). For several years it was these textbooks and Mao's 'Little Red Book' that constituted our only source of intellectual knowledge. All other books were forbidden.

First we were refused admission to high school, then the role of young intellectuals was foisted on us on account of our parents being labelled 'enemies of the people'.

My parents were doctors. My father was a lung specialist, and my mother a consultant in parasitic diseases. Both of them worked at the hospital of Chengdu, a city of four million inhabitants. Their crime was that they were 'stinking scientific authorities' who enjoyed a modest reputation on a provincial scale, Chengdu being the capital of Szechuan, a province with a population of one hundred million. Far away from Beijing but very close to Tibet.

Compared with my parents, Luo's father, a famous dentist whose name was known all over China, was a real celebrity. One day – this was before the Cultural Revolution – he mentioned to his students that he had fixed Mao Zedong's teeth as well as those of Madame Mao and Jiang Jieshi, who had been president of the Republic prior to the Communist takeover. There were those who, having contemplated Mao's portrait every day for years, had indeed noted that his teeth looked remarkably stained, not to say yellow, but no one said so out loud. And yet here was an eminent dentist stating publicly that the Great Helmsman of the Revolution had been fitted with new teeth, just like that. It was beyond belief, an unpardonable, insane crime, worse than revealing a secret of national security. His crime was all the more grave because he dared to mention the names of Mao and his consort in the same breath as that of the worst scum of the earth: Jiang Jieshi.

For many years Luo's family lived in the apartment next to ours, on the third and top floor of a brick building. He was the fifth son of his father, and the only child of his mother.

I am not exaggerating when I say that Luo was the best friend I ever had. We grew up together, we shared all sorts of experiences, often tough ones. We very rarely quarrelled.

I will never forget the one time we came to blows, or rather the time he hit me. It was in the summer of 1968. He was about fifteen, I had just turned fourteen. That afternoon a big political meeting was being held on the sports ground of the hospital where our parents worked. Both of us were aware that the butt of the rally would be Luo's father, that yet another public humiliation awaited him. When it was nearly five o'clock and no one had yet returned, Luo asked me to accompany him to the hospital.

'We'll note down everyone who denounces my father, or beats him,' he said. 'That way we can take our revenge when we're older.'

The sports ground was a bobbing sea of dark heads. It was a very hot day. Loudspeakers blared. Luo's father was on his hands and knees in front of a grandstand. A great slab of cement hung round his neck from a wire so deeply embedded in the skin as to be invisible. Written on the slab were his name and his crime: REACTIONARY.

Even from where I was standing, thirty metres away, I could make out a dark stain on the ground made by the sweat dripping from his brow.

A man's voice roared through the loudspeaker.

'Admit that you slept with the nurse!'

Luo's father hung his head, so low that his face seemed buried in the cement slab. A microphone was shoved under his mouth and a faint, tremulous 'yes' was heard.

'Tell us what happened!' the inquisitor's voice barked from the loudspeaker. 'Who started it?'

'I did.'

'And then?'

A few seconds of silence ensued. Then the whole crowd screamed in unison: 'And then?'

This cry, raised by two thousand voices, was like the rumble of thunder breaking over our heads.

'I started it . . .' Luo's father confessed.

'Go on! The details!'

'But as soon as I touched her, I fell . . . into mist and clouds.'

We left as the crowd of fanatics resumed their mass inquisition. On the way home I suddenly felt tears running down my cheeks, and I realised how fond I was of the dentist.

At that moment, without saying a word, Luo punched me. I was so taken aback that I nearly lost my balance.

IN 1971 there was little to distinguish us two – one the son of a pulmonary specialist, the other the son of a notorious class enemy who had enjoyed the privilege of touching Mao's teeth – from the other hundred-odd 'young intellectuals' who were banished to the mountain known as the Phoenix of the Sky. The name was a poetic way of suggesting its terrifying altitude; the poor sparrows and common birds of the plain could never soar to its peak, for that was the reserve of winged creatures allied to the sky: mighty, mythical and profoundly solitary.

There was no road into the mountain, only a narrow pathway threading steeply through great walls of craggy rock. For a glimpse of a car, the sound of a horn, a whiff of restaurant food, indeed for any sign of civilisation, you had to tramp across rugged mountain terrain for two days. A hundred kilometres later you would reach the banks of the River Ya and the small town of Yong Jing. The only Westerner ever to have set foot here was a French missionary, Father Michel, who tried to find a new route to Tibet in the 1940s.

'The district of Yong Jing is not lacking in interest,' the

Jesuit commented in his notebook. 'One of the mountains, locally known as "the Phoenix of the Sky", is especially noteworthy. Famed for its copper, employed by the ancients for minting coins, the mountain is said to have been offered by an emperor of the Han dynasty as a gift to his favourite, who was one of the chief eunuchs in his palace. Looking up at the vertiginous slopes all around me, I could just make out a footpath rising from the shadowy fissures in the cliff towards the sky, where it seemed to melt into the misty air. I noted a small band of coolies making their way down this path, laden like beasts of burden with great panniers of copper tied to their backs. I am told that the production of copper has been in decline for many years, primarily due to the difficulty of transport. At present, the peculiar geographic conditions of the mountain have led the local population to grow opium. I have been advised against climbing it, as all the opium growers are armed. After harvesting their crop, they spend their time attacking anyone who happens to pass by. So I content myself with observing from afar this wild and lonely place, so thickly screened by giant trees, tangled creepers and lush vegetation as to make one expect to see a bandit leaping from the shadows at any moment.'

The Phoenix of the Sky comprised some twenty villages scattered along the single serpentine footpath or hidden in the depths of gloomy valleys. Usually each village took in five or six young people from the city. But our village, perched on the summit and the poorest of them all, could only afford two: Luo and me. We were assigned quarters in the very house on stilts where the village headman had inspected my violin. This building was village property, and had not been constructed with habitation in mind. Underneath, in the space between the wooden props supporting the floor, was a pigsty occupied by a large, plump sow – likewise common property. The structure itself was made of rough wooden planks, the walls were unpainted and the beams exposed; it was more like a barn for the storage of maize, rice and tools in need of repair. It was also a perfect trysting place for adulterous lovers.

Throughout the years of our re-education the house on stilts remained almost entirely unfurnished. There was not even a table or chair, just two makeshift beds pushed against the wall in a small windowless alcove.

Nonetheless, our home soon became the focal point of the village, thanks to another phoenix, a smaller version, miniature almost, and rather more earthbound, whose master was my friend Luo.

Actually, it wasn't really a phoenix but a proud rooster with peacock-like feathers of shimmering green with flashes of deep blue. Under the somewhat dusty glass cover of Luo's alarm clock it could be seen pecking an invisible floor with its sharp ebony beak, while the second hand crept slowly round the clock face. Then it would raise its head, open its beak wide and shake its plumage, visibly gratified, sated with imaginary grains of rice.

It was a tiny clock and it was no doubt thanks to its size that it had escaped the notice of the village headman when we arrived. It fitted in the palm of your hand, and tinkled prettily when the alarm went off.

Before our arrival, there had never been an alarm clock in the village, indeed there had been no clocks or watches at all. The people had timed their days by sunrise and sundown.

We were surprised to see how the alarm clock seized the imagination of the peasants. It became an object of veneration, almost. Everyone came to consult the clock, as though our house on stilts were a temple. Every morning saw the same ritual: the village headman would pace to and fro, smoking his bamboo pipe, which was as long as an old-fashioned rifle, all the while keeping a watchful eye on the clock. At nine o'clock sharp he would give a long piercing whistle to summon the villagers to work in the fields.

'It's time! Do you hear?' he would shout, dead on cue, at the surrounding houses. 'Time to get off your backsides, you lazy louts, you spawn of bullocks' balls! What are you waiting for?'

Neither Luo nor I could muster any enthusiasm for the work we were forced to do on this mountain with its tortuous paths rising ever higher until they vanished into the clouds, paths not wide enough even for a hand cart, so that the human body represented the sole means of transport.

What we dreaded most of all was having to carry buckets of shit on our backs. These wooden buckets were semi-cylindrical in shape, and designed specifically for the transportation of all manner of waste, whether human or animal. Each day we had to fill the 'back-buckets' with a mixture of excrement and water, hoist them onto our shoulders and clamber up the mountainside to the fields, many of which were situated at dizzying heights. With each step we could hear the liquid sewage sloshing in the bucket, just behind our ears. The slurry would seep through the lid and trickle down our bodies until we were soaked. Dear reader, I will spare you the details of each faltering step; suffice it to say that the slightest false move was potentially fatal.

One morning when we woke, the thought of the back-buckets awaiting us was so dispiriting that we couldn't bring ourselves to get up. We were still in bed when we heard the village headman's footsteps approaching. It was nearly nine o'clock, and at the sight of the rooster dutifully pecking away Luo had a brainwave: with his little finger he slid the hands of the clock back by one hour. We got back into bed to enjoy our lie-in, which was all the sweeter knowing that the village headman was pacing to and fro outside, puffing on his long bamboo pipe. The sheer audacity of our trick did a lot to temper our resentment against the former opium growers who, now that they had been converted into 'poor peasants' by the Communist regime, were in charge of our re-education.

After that historic morning we got into the habit of readjusting the time on the alarm clock. It all depended on how we were feeling, physically and mentally. Sometimes, instead of turning the clock back, we would put it forward by an hour or two, so as to finish the day's work early.

In the end we had changed the position of the hands so many times that we had no idea what the time really was.

It rained often on Phoenix mountain. It rained almost two days out of three. Storms or torrential downpours were rare; instead there was a steady, insidious drizzle that seemed to go on for ever and the peaks and cliffs surrounding our house on stilts were constantly veiled in a thick, sinister mist. The unearthly panorama depressed us. What with the perpetual humidity inside the hut and the ever more oppressive damp in the walls, it was worse than living in a cellar.

Luo would sometimes be unable to sleep. He would get up, light the oil lamp, and crawl under his bed to hunt for any stray cigarette butts he might have forgotten about.

When he re-emerged from the shadows he would sit cross-legged on top of the bed, and pile the damp butts on a scrap of paper (often a precious letter from his family) and dry them over the oil lamp. Then he would gather together the flakes of tobacco with the precision of a watchmaker, without missing a single strand. Having rolled his cigarette, he would extinguish the lamp and sit and smoke in the dark, listening to the silence of the night broken only by the muffled grunts coming from below, where the sow was rooting busily in the mire.

From time to time the rain lasted for days on end, and the lack of tobacco would become increasingly irksome. On one occasion Luo woke me up in the middle of the night.

'I can't find a single fag end.'

'So?'

'I feel depressed,' he said. 'Why don't you play me something on your violin?'

I did as he said. Raising my bow, still half asleep, I suddenly thought of our parents, his and mine: if only they could have seen the wavering light of the oil lamp in our house on stilts, if only they could have heard the strains of my violin interspersed with the grunts of the sow . . . But there was no one to hear. Not even a villager. Our nearest neighbour was at least a hundred metres away.

Outside, it was raining. Not the usual fine drizzle as it happened, but a heavy downpour drumming on the tiles overhead. No doubt this exacerbated Luo's gloom: it felt as if we were doomed to spend our entire lives being re-educated. Ordinarily the offspring of average parents, whether workers or revolutionary intellectuals, could rest assured that, provided they stayed out of trouble, they would be reunited with their families after a mere two years of re-education. That was the official Party line. But for the sons and daughters of families classed as enemies of the people, the chances of returning home were infinitesimal: three in a thousand. Statistically speaking, Luo and I were no-hopers. We were left with the dismal prospect of growing old and bald in the house on stilts, and of dying there too, after which our bodies would be wrapped in the white shrouds typical of the region. There was plenty of cause for dejection and insomnia.

That night I played a piece by Mozart, some Brahms, and finally a Beethoven sonata, but even that failed to raise my friend's spirits.

'Try something else,' he said.

'Any ideas?'

'Something a bit more cheerful.'

I thought hard, running through my scant musical repertoire, but came up with nothing.

Luo started humming a revolutionary tune.

'How does that strike you?' he asked.

'Charming.'

I launched into an accompaniment on my violin. It was a Tibetan song, which the Chinese had reworded so as to turn it into a glorification of Chairman Mao. But the adaptation of the lyrics had not done too much damage: the song was still uplifting. With mounting excitement Luo scrambled to his feet and started jumping up and down on his bed, to the steady patter of the rain dripping down through the broken tiles.

'Three in a thousand', flashed across my mind. I had a three in a thousand chance, and our melancholy smoker here, currently disguised as a dancer, stood even less of a chance. Some day, perhaps, once I was an accomplished violinist, some modest local or regional propaganda committee – in the district of Yong Jing, for instance – might open their doors to me, and might even hire me to perform Red violin concertos. But Luo couldn't play the violin, I reflected, and he wasn't much good at basketball or football either. In fact he didn't possess a single skill that might help him to become one of the three in a thousand. He couldn't even dream of it.

The only thing Luo was really good at was telling stories. A pleasing talent to be sure, but a marginal one, with little future in it. Modern man has moved beyond the age of the Thousand-And-One-Nights, and modern societies everywhere, whether socialist or capitalist, have done away with the old storytellers – more's the pity.

The only man in the world who truly appreciated his gift, to the point of rewarding him generously, was the headman of our village, the last of the lordly devotees of narrative eloquence.

Phoenix mountain was so remote from civilisation that most of the inhabitants had never had the opportunity of seeing a film, let alone visit a cinema. There had been a few occasions when Luo and I entertained the headman with stories of films we had seen, and he was eager to hear more. One day, having found out when the next month's screening was due at Yong Jing, he decided to send Luo and me to watch it. We got two days off for the journey to town and two for the return, and we were supposed to see the show on the evening of our arrival. Back home in the village we were to relate the film from beginning to end to the headman and everyone else, and to make our story last exactly as long as the screen version.

We welcomed the challenge, and to be on the safe side we sat through two screenings in succession. The basketball court of the town's high school had been converted into a makeshift open-air cinema. The local girls were gorgeous, but we forced ourselves to concentrate on the screen, paying close attention to the dialogue, to the actors' costumes and gestures, to the setting of every scene, even to the music.

On our return to the village we put on an 'oral cinema show' such as had never been seen before. Every single villager was crammed into the clearing in front of our house on stilts. The headman sat in the middle of the front row, holding his long bamboo pipe in one hand and our 'phoenix of the earth' in the other, to time the duration of our performance.

I was overcome by stagefright and was reduced to a mechanical recitation of the setting of each scene. But here Luo's genius for storytelling came into its own. He was sparing with his descriptions, but acted the part of each character in turn, adjusting his tone of voice and gestures accordingly. He took complete control of the narrative, keeping up the suspense, asking the listeners questions, making them respond and correcting their answers. By the time we, or rather he, reached the end of the story in the alloted time, our audience was ecstatic.

'Next month,' the village headman announced with an imperious smile, 'I shall send you to another film. You will be paid the same as if you had worked in the fields.'

At first we thought it would just be a welcome change; not for a moment did we imagine that our lives, particularly Luo's, were about to be completely shaken up.

THE PRINCESS of Phoenix mountain wore pale pink canvas shoes which were both sturdy and supple, and through which you could see her flexing her toes as she worked the treadle of her sewing machine. There was nothing out of the ordinary about the cheap, home-made shoes, and yet, in a place where nearly everyone went barefoot, they caught the eye, seemed delicate and sophisticated. The fine shape of her feet and ankles was set off by white nylon socks.

A long pigtail three or four centimetres wide fell from the nape of her neck down to the small of her back, where the end was tied with a brand-new red silk ribbon.

When she leaned over her sewing machine, the shiny metal base mirrored the collar of her white blouse, her oval face, and the sparkle in her eyes – without doubt the loveliest pair of eyes in the district of Yong Jing, if not the entire region.

A steep valley divided her village from ours. Her father, the only tailor on the mountain, was often absent from their home, which was old and spacious and served as both shop and dwelling. His tailoring was much in demand.

Whenever a family needed new clothes they would first go all the way to Yong Jing to buy lengths of cloth, after which they would visit the tailor to discuss styles, prices and a convenient date for him to come and make the garments. On the appointed day an escort party would call for him at dawn, with several strong men to take turns carrying the sewing machine on their backs.

The tailor owned two sewing machines. The first, which he took with him from one village to the next, was old: the brand and name of the manufacturer were no longer legible. The second was new, *Made in Shanghai*, and he left it at home for his daughter, 'the Little Seamstress'. He never took his daughter with him on his trips, and this decision, prudent but pitiless, caused great distress to all the young bachelors aspiring to win her favour.

The tailor lived like a king. Wherever he went there would be scenes of excitement to rival a country festival. The home of his client, filled with the whirr of his sewing machine, would become the hub of village life, giving the host family the opportunity to display their wealth. He would be served the choicest food, and sometimes, if the year was drawing to a close and preparations for the New Year celebrations were under way, a pig might even be slaughtered. He would often spend a week or two in a village, lodging with each of his diverse clients in succession.

Luo and I first met the tailor when we went to visit Four-Eyes, a friend from the old days who had been sent to another village. It was raining, and we had to walk carefully along the steep, slippery path shrouded in milky fog. Despite our caution we found ourselves on all fours in the mud several times. Suddenly, as we rounded a corner, we saw coming towards us a procession in single file, accompanying a sedan chair in which a middle-aged man was enthroned. Following behind this regal conveyance was a porter with a sewing machine strapped to his back. The man bent to address his bearers, and seemed to be enquiring about us.

He was of slight build, thin, wrinkled, but brimming with energy. His sedan was lashed to two sturdy bamboo shafts which rested on the shoulders of two bearers, one in front and one behind. We could hear the chair and the shafts creaking to the rhythm of the bearers' slow, heavy tread.

When we were about to pass the sedan, the tailor leaned over to me, so close that I could feel his breath: 'Wy-o-lin!' he bellowed, in an imitation of the English word.

His voice was like a clap of thunder and made me jump, at which he roared with laughter. He was the very image of a capricious overlord.

'Do you realise that here, on this mountain, our tailor is the most widely travelled man of all?' one of the bearers asked.

'In my youth I even went as far as Ya An, which is two hundred kilometres away from Yong Jing,' the great traveller declared before we had a chance to reply. 'When I was young my master had a musical instrument just like yours up on his wall, to impress his clients.'

Then he fell silent, and the procession set off again.

Just before he disappeared from view, he turned and shouted once more: 'Wy-o-lin!'

His bearers and the ten peasants escorting him slowly raised their heads and let out a long drawn-out cry, so deformed that it sounded more like an anguished wail than an English word.

'Wy-o-lin!'

Like a pack of mischievous boys they fell about laughing. Then they bowed their heads and went on their way. Very soon the procession was swallowed up by the fog.

Some weeks later we ventured into the courtyard of his house, where a large black dog stared at us but did not bark. We entered the shop. The old man being away on one of his tours, we were greeted by his daughter, the Little Seamstress. We asked her to lengthen Luo's trousers by five centimetres; even his poor diet, insomnia, and constant worrying about the future had not stopped him from growing.

Introducing himself to the Little Seamstress, Luo told her about our encounter with her father in the fog and the rain, and he couldn't resist imitating and exaggerating the old man's funny English accent. She hooted with laughter. Luo was a born impersonator.

When she laughed I noticed an untamed quality about her eyes, which reminded me of the wild girls on our side of the mountain. Her eyes had the gleam of uncut gems, of unpolished metal, which was heightened by the long lashes and the delicate slant of the lids.

'You mustn't mind him,' she said. 'He's just an overgrown child.'

Her face clouded suddenly, and she lowered her eyes. She scratched the base of her sewing machine with a fingertip.

'My mother died far too young. Ever since her passing he has done exactly as he pleases.'

She had a glowing complexion and her features were fine, almost noble. Her face possessed an impressive, sensual beauty, which aroused in us an irresistible desire to

23

stay and watch her work the treadle of her *Made in Shanghai*.

The room served as shop, work place and dining room all at once. The floorboards were grimy and streaked with yellow and black gobs of dried spittle left by clients. You could tell they were not washed down daily. There were hangers with finished garments suspended on a string across the middle of the room. The corners were piled high with bolts of material and folded clothes, which were under siege from an army of ants. The place lacked any sense of order or aesthetics, and emanated an atmosphere of complete informality.

I was surprised to see a book lying on a table, since the mountain people were mostly illiterate; it was an eternity since I had touched the pages of a book. I went to look at it at once, but was disappointed: it was an industrial catalogue of textile dyes.

'Can you read?' I asked.

'Not much,' she answered, unabashed. 'But you needn't think I'm a fool, because I enjoy talking to people who can read and write – the young people from the city, for instance. Didn't you notice that my dog didn't bark when you came in? He knows my tastes.'

She didn't seem to want us to leave just yet. She rose from her stool, lit the iron stove in the centre of the room, set a saucepan on the burner and filled it with water. Luo, who followed her every move with his eyes, asked: 'Are you intending to offer us tea or boiling water?'

'It'll be the latter.'

This was a sign that she had taken a liking to us. On this mountain an invitation to take a drink of water meant that your host would crack some eggs over the boiling pan and add sugar to make a soup.

'Did you know, Little Seamstress,' Luo said, 'that you and I have something in common?'

'Us two?'

'Yes, you want to bet?'

'What shall we bet?'

'Whatever you like. I'm quite sure I can prove to you that there's something we share.'

She reflected briefly.

'If I lose, I'll lengthen your trousers for free.'

'Fine,' said Luo. 'Now take off your left shoe and sock.'

After a moment's hesitation the Little Seamstress's curiosity got the better of her. Her foot, more timid than she but no less sensual for that, gradually revealed itself. A small foot, tanned, translucent, veined with blue, with toenails that gleamed.

Luo planted his bony, mud-encrusted foot alongside hers, and it was true, there was a resemblance: their second toes were longer than the others.

It was a long journey home, so we set out around three o'clock in the afternoon in order to reach our village before nightfall.

On the way I asked Luo: 'D'you fancy her, the Little Seamstress?'

He plodded on with bowed head, taking his time to reply.

'Have you fallen in love with her?' I persisted.

'She's not civilised, at least not enough for me!'

A PINPRICK of light quivered in the darkness at the end of a long subterranean passage. The tiny bright dot wavered, fell, rose again, and continued its precarious advance. Now and then, when there was a dip in the floor, the dot disappeared for seconds at a time. The silence was broken only by the scraping of a heavy basket being hauled over the ground and the grunts of a man exerting himself to his limits. The sound reverberated in the inky tunnel, generating an echo that travelled great distances.

When the light suddenly reappeared, it hovered in the air like the eye of some nightmarish animal whose body had been swallowed up by the darkness.

It was Luo, wearing an oil lamp secured to his forehead, at work in what was known as 'the little coal mine'. Where the passage was too low he had to get down on all fours and crawl. He was naked except for a harness with leather straps that cut deep into his flesh. This horrible contraption enabled him to drag a huge basket laden with chunks of anthracite behind him.

When he reached me I took over from him. I was

naked too, my body covered in a film of coal dust which sank into every fold of my skin. I preferred to push the basket instead of pulling it behind me as he did. Close to the pit face there was a sizeable ramp, but the ceiling was higher there; Luo would often help me work my cargo to the top and out of the tunnel. We would drop to the ground from exhaustion in the great cloud of dust raised by tipping the contents of the basket onto the coal heap.

In olden times the Phoenix of the Sky, as we have seen, was famed for its copper mines (which earned a place in Chinese history for having been given away in a generous gesture by China's first official homosexual, an emperor). Though the copper mines had fallen into disuse and ruin, coal mining continued on a small, manual scale. The coal mines were collectively owned by all the peasants on the mountain, and were exploited to meet the local demand for fuel. So it was hardly surprising that Luo and I, like the other city youths, were put to work underground for two months as part of our re-education. Even the success of our oral cinema show didn't earn us a dispensation.

To tell the truth, we accepted this infernal ordeal, because we were determined to stay in the race at all costs, even though our chances of returning to the city were no more than the infinitesimal three in a thousand. We were not to know that our stint in the coal mine would mark us for the rest of our lives, physically and especially mentally. Even today the fearful phrase 'the little coal mine' sends shivers down my spine.

With the exception of the entrance, where there was a section about twenty metres long with a low ceiling supported by ill-fitting beams and props made of rough-hewn tree trunks, the tunnel, all seven hundred metres of it, lacked any protection whatsoever. There was a permanent danger of falling rock, and the three old peasant-miners whose job it was to hack at the coal seams were forever telling us of the fatal accidents that had befallen our predecessors.

Each basketful that we managed to haul all the way from the end of the tunnel became a game of Russian roulette.

One day, as we were heaving a full basket of coal up the final steep incline, I heard Luo say: 'I don't know why, but from the moment we got here I've had this idea stuck in my head: that I'm going to die in this mine.'

Hearing this, my breath failed me. We continued climbing, but I suddenly broke out in a cold sweat. I had become infected by the same idea as Luo: from that day on I shared his terror of not leaving the place alive.

During our time at the mine, Luo and I slept in the peasants' dormitory, a humble cabin clinging to the mountainside under a rocky outcrop. Waking up in the morning, I would hear the rain dripping from the rock onto the cabin roof, which was covered with bits of tree bark, and would console myself with the thought that at least I was still alive. But each morning when leaving the cabin I was terrified that I would not make it back there at night. The most trivial occurrence, someone's offhand remark, for instance, or a macabre joke, or just a change in the weather, became, in my eyes, a bad omen, a foreboding of death.

I had visions, sometimes, while I was at work in the mine. The ground would become soft, I would have difficulty breathing and would feel as if I were on the brink of death, whereupon I saw my childhood race before me at breakneck speed, the way the dying are said to see their lives pass by in a flash. The rubbery ground stretched elastically with each step I took, then there was a deafening roar overhead as if the roof were about to cave in. Crazed with fear I would get down on my hands and knees and crawl in the dark with my mother and father's faces looming before my eyes. The vision lasted a few seconds, then it vanished as suddenly as it had come, leaving me in the desolation of the mine shaft, naked as a worm, struggling to heave my burden towards the exit. I fastened my eyes on the ground at my feet: in the flickering light of my pit lamp I caught sight of a forlorn ant. It was advancing slowly and steadily, driven by the will to survive.

One day – it was during our third week there – I heard someone sobbing in the tunnel, but saw no light at all.

It did not sound like grief, nor like the groans of a wounded man; it was more like someone weeping with passionate abandon. The sound bounced off the walls and echoed all the way to the other end of the shaft before subsiding into the shadows. I was sure it was Luo who was crying in the dark.

At the end of the sixth week Luo fell ill. It was malaria. One afternoon, when we were all sitting under a tree opposite the entrance to the tunnel eating some rice, he complained of feeling cold. Within minutes his hands were shaking so badly he couldn't hold his chopsticks. He rose unsteadily to his feet and headed back to the dormitory to lie down, but could barely walk. His eyes were glazed. Standing before the open door of the cabin, he called out to no one in particular: 'Let me in!' This was met with roars of laughter from the miners eating their rice under the tree.

'Who are you talking to?' they wanted to know. 'There's no one there.'

In the cabin that night he was still complaining of the cold, despite several quilts and the coals burning in the big stove.

The men launched into a long discussion, in hushed voices. They debated whether they should take Luo to the river and dunk him in the icy water, without telling him beforehand. They thought the shock would cure him. However, this proposal was turned down, for fear of seeing him drown in the middle of the night.

One of the men went outside and returned holding two branches. 'One from a peach tree, the other from a willow,' he told me. Only these trees would do. He hauled Luo to his feet, stripped him of his jacket and other clothing, and started whipping his bare back with the two branches.

'Harder!' cried the others, watching from the sidelines. 'If you don't hit hard you won't drive out the sickness.'

The branches whistled through the air as they swung, one after the other. The blows left livid weals on Luo's flesh but my friend underwent the flogging impassively. Although he was conscious, it was as though he were in a dream where it was all happening to someone else. I couldn't tell what he was thinking, but I was very anxious, and the remark he had made in the mine shaft a few weeks before came back to me, reverberating in the cruel whoosh of the branches: 'I've had this idea stuck in my head: that I'm going to die in this mine.'

The man wielding the branches grew tired and asked for someone else to take over. But no one came forward. Overcome with fatigue, the men had gone to their bunks and wanted to sleep. I found myself holding the branches of peach and willow. Luo raised his head. His face was pale and his forehead beaded with perspiration. His eyes had a faraway look when they met mine.

'Go on,' he said, in a voice that was barely audible.

'Shouldn't you take a rest?' I asked. 'Look how your hands are trembling. Are they numb?'

'Yes they are,' he said, raising one hand to his eyes for inspection. 'You're right, I'm shivering and I'm cold, like an old man at death's door.'

I found a fag end in the bottom of my pocket, which I lit and offered to him. But it slipped from his fingers at once and fell to the ground.

'Too damn heavy,' he said.

'D'you really want me to go on flogging you?'

'Yes, it'll warm me up.'

Before complying with his wish I thought I would retrieve the fallen cigarette and let him have a good smoke first. I bent over to pick up the fag end, which was still alight. Suddenly I spied something whitish lying on the floor by the foot of the bed: it was an envelope.

I picked it up. The envelope, which was addressed to Luo, had not been opened. I asked the men where it came from. One of them replied from his bunk that it had been left earlier in the day by someone come to buy coal.

I opened it. Inside I found a letter written in pencil. The characters were not evenly disposed on the page and some of them were poorly drawn, yet the erratic writing gave the impression of feminine sweetness, of child-like sincerity. I read it out to Luo slowly:

To Luo the teller of films.
Don't laugh at my handwriting. Unlike you, I did not attend middle school. You know that the nearest school is located in the town of Yong Jing, and that it takes two days to get there from the

mountain. I was taught to read and write by my father. You can class me among 'those who have completed elementary education'.

I heard not long ago that you and your friend are very good at relating what happens in films. I have been to see the headman of my village, and he has agreed to send two farm workers to the little mine to take your place for a couple of days. Now you can come to our village to tell us a film.

I wanted to go up to the mine to bring you the news myself, but was told that the men all go about naked there, and that the place is forbidden for girls.

Thinking of the coal mine, I admire your courage. I keep my fingers crossed that it won't cave in. You'll be getting two days off: at least you won't be at risk during that time.

See you soon. Say hello to your friend the fiddler.

The Little Seamstress

08.07.1972

P.S. I just remembered something funny I wanted to tell you: since your visit I've come across several people whose second toes are longer than their big toes, just like ours. I'm disappointed, but that's life.

WE OPTED for the story of *The Little Flower Seller*. By now we had seen three films at the basketball court in Yong Jing. By far the most popular was a North Korean melodrama with a heroine called 'the Flower Girl'. We had already told the story in our village, and when we came to the end of the performance I imitated the sentimental, throaty voice-over I had heard in town – 'The saying goes: a sincere heart can make even a stone blossom. So tell me, was the flower girl's heart lacking in sincerity?' The effect had been as grandiose as that of the screen version. The whole audience wept, even the village headman who, for all his harshness, couldn't hold back the tears pouring hotly from his left eye, marked as ever by three spots of blood.

Although Luo was suffering from recurrent bouts of fever, he claimed he was already well enough for us to undertake the journey to the village where the Little Seamstress lived. He set off with the confident air of a conqueror. However, he was struck down by another attack of malaria on the way.

Although the sun was shining brightly, he said he could

feel the cold creeping up on him. I managed to light a fire with some twigs and dead leaves, and made him sit next to it, but instead of warming up he felt colder than ever.

'Let's press on,' he said, struggling to his feet. (His teeth were chattering.)

All along the pathway we could hear the rush of a mountain torrent and the cries of monkeys and other wild creatures. Luo was alternately excruciatingly cold and unbearably hot. Now and then he would teeter so close to the edge of the precipice that he dislodged stones and clods of earth. The sound of them hitting the bottom of the ravine took an eternity to reach our ears. At such times I would persuade him to rest a while until the fever subsided.

Upon arriving at the Little Seamstress's home, we were pleased to learn that her father was on one of his trips. Like the first time, the black dog came to snuffle at our legs but did not bark.

Luo's face was flushed a deep crimson: he was delirious. The Little Seamstress was shocked to see the ravages wrought by his fevers. She promptly cancelled the oral cinema show and installed Luo in her room, on her bed under a white mosquito net. She rolled her long pigtail into a high chignon on the top of her head. Then she took off her pink shoes and ran outside, barefoot.

'Why don't you come along?' she called out to me. 'I know a very good remedy for him.'

It was a common plant, growing on the banks of a little stream, not far from her village. Bushy, barely thirty centimetres high, it had bright pink flowers with petals resembling outsize peach blossom, which were reflected in the limpid, shallow water of the stream. The medicinal properties were concentrated in the angular, spiky leaves shaped like ducks' feet, of which the Little Seamstress gathered large quantities.

'What's the name of this plant?' I asked her.

'It's called "Broken-bowl-shards".'

She pounded the leaves in a white stone mortar until they were reduced to a thick greenish paste, which she proceeded to smear on Luo's left wrist. Although still feverish, he had recovered a certain rationality and willingly let her apply the poultice. She bound it up with a long strip of white linen.

Towards nightfall Luo's breathing calmed somewhat, and he fell asleep.

'D'you believe in that sort of thing?' the Little Seamstress asked me in a hesitant voice.

'What sort of thing?'

'Things you can't explain naturally.'

'Sometimes I do, sometimes I don't.'

'You sound as if you think I'll denounce you.'

'Not at all.'

'Well?'

'In my opinion you can't believe in them totally, but you can't deny them totally either.'

She seemed to approve of my answer. Glancing at Luo asleep on her bed she asked: 'What is Luo's father? A Buddhist?'

'I don't know. But he's a famous dentist.'

'What's a dentist?'

'Don't you know what a dentist is? Dentists take care of your teeth.'

'Really? You mean to say that they can kill the worms that get into your teeth and make them ache?'

'That's right,' I replied, without laughing. 'I'll tell you a secret, but you must swear you'll never tell another soul.'

'I swear . . .'

'His father,' I said, lowering my voice, 'got rid of all the worms in Chairman Mao's teeth.'

After a moment's respectful silence, she asked: 'If I got the sorceresses to come and keep a vigil by his son's sickbed tonight, would he mind?'

Towards midnight four old crones arrived from three different villages. They wore trailing robes of black and blue, flowers in their hair and jade bracelets on their wrists. The sorceresses huddled over Luo, who was twitching in his sleep. Then they settled down at the four corners of the bed and eyed him through the mosquito net. It was hard to say which of them was the most ugly and likely to frighten off evil spirits.

One of the sorceresses, the most shrivelled of all, held a bow and arrow in her hands.

'I can guarantee,' she said to me, 'that the evil spirit of the little coal mine, the one who's been plaguing your friend here, won't dare to come tonight. My bow is from Tibet, and my arrow is tipped with silver. When I shoot my arrow it whistles in the air like a flying flute, and never fails to pierce the breast of demons, however powerful they may be.'

Not only were the sorceresses very old, it was also very late, and after a while they began to yawn. And despite the strong tea our hostess plied them with, they nodded off, one after the other. The owner of the bow, too, succumbed to sleep: she laid the weapon on the bed and her slack, painted lids drooped heavily and closed.

'Wake them up,' the Little Seamstress said to me. 'Tell them a film.'

'What kind?'

'Doesn't matter. Just keep them awake . . .'

So I embarked on the strangest performance of my life. In that remote village tucked into a cleft in the mountain where my friend had fallen into a sort of stupor, I sat in the flickering light of an oil lamp and related the North Korean film for the benefit of a pretty girl and four ancient sorceresses.

I got along on my own as best I could. After a few minutes the audience was captivated by the story of the poor flower girl. They even asked questions, and the longer I spoke the less they had to blink their eyes to stay awake.

Still, the magic was not the same as when Luo took the lead. I was not a born storyteller. We were different. Half an hour into the story the flower girl, having gone to extreme lengths to get some money, rushes to the hospital only to find that she is too late: her mother has died, calling desperately for her daughter in her last breath. A propaganda film like any other. Normally speaking, the deathbed scene marked the first high point in the story. The audience would always weep at this moment, regardless of whether they were watching the film or listening to our version of it. Perhaps the sorceresses were made of different stuff. They listened attentively, with some degree of engagement – I could even sense a slight frisson of emotion – but no tears were shed.

Disappointed by the effect of my performance, I dwelt on the description of the flower girl's uncontrollably shaking hand and the bank notes slipping from her fingers . . . But the sorceresses were unimpressed.

Suddenly, from inside the white mosquito net, came a voice that sounded as if it issued from the bottom of a well.

'The saying goes,' Luo intoned, 'that a sincere heart can

make a stone blossom. So tell me, was the flower girl's heart lacking in sincerity?'

I was struck more by the fact that Luo had uttered the resounding finale before the story had ended than by his sudden awakening. But what a surprise, when I glanced around the room: the four sorceresses were weeping! Their tears spurted forth generously and coursed down their warped, fissured cheeks.

How great Luo's talent was! He was able to electrify an audience by means of a perfectly timed voice-over, even when overcome by a violent bout of malaria.

As I continued with the story, I had the impression there was something different about the Little Seamstress and I realised that her hair was hanging loose in luxuriant tresses, a wonderful mane cascading over her shoulders. I guessed that Luo must have reached out of the mosquito net and untied her long pigtail with his feverish fingers. A sudden draught made the lamp sputter and die, and in that moment I thought I saw the Little Seamstress lift one corner of the net and bend over Luo in the dark for a furtive kiss.

One of the sorceresses relit the oil lamp, and I went on to tell the rest of the Korean girl's sad story. The sorceresses wept profusely, their tears mingling with the phlegm running from their nostrils, and their snuffling continued until deep into the night.

PART II

FOUR-EYES had a secret suitcase, which he kept carefully hidden.

He was our friend. (Remember? We were on our way to see him when we had our encounter with the tailor on the mountain path.) The village where Four-Eyes was being re-educated was situated lower on the slopes of Phoenix mountain than ours. Luo and I often went over to his house in the evening to cook a meal if we had managed to lay hands on a bit of meat, a bottle of local liquor, or some fresh vegetables from the peasants' gardens. We would share our spoils, as if we were a gang of three. This made it all the more surprising that he didn't breathe a word to us about his mysterious suitcase.

His family lived in the same city as our parents: his father was a writer, his mother a poet. Recently disgraced by the authorities, they had burdened their beloved son with the same dreaded odds as Luo and I faced: the terrible three in a thousand. So we were all in the same boat, but Four-Eyes, who was eighteen years old at the time, lived in almost perpetual fear.

In his presence everything became tinged with danger.

At his house we felt like three criminals huddling conspiratorially around the oil lamp. Take the meal, for instance: a knock on the door while we were wreathed in the delicious aromas of some meat dish we had prepared (cooking smells that plunged the three of us, famished, into a frenzy of anticipation) was enough to frighten him out of his wits. He would spring to his feet, quickly hide the pan in a corner as if it were contraband, and put out a dish of marinated vegetables, mushy and repulsive, in its stead: eating meat struck him a crime typical of the bourgeois class to which his family belonged.

The day after my performance for the four sorceresses, Luo felt a little better. He was well enough to go home, he said, and the Little Seamstress didn't insist on our staying. I imagine she was exhausted.

After breakfast, we set off along the lonely mountain footpath. The damp morning air felt pleasantly refreshing on our flushed faces. Luo smoked as he walked. At first the path descended a little way, then it rose again. When it got steep, I took my sick friend's arm. The ground was soft and wet; the trees intertwined their branches overhead. Passing the village where Four-Eyes lived, we spotted him at work in a paddy field. He was tilling the soil with the aid of a plough and a water buffalo.

We could not see the furrows he was making because the thick fertile bed was flooded with flat water. Bare from the waist up, our friend was making slow progress, for with each step he sank down to his knees in the thick mud while the black buffalo strained at the plough. The slanting rays of the early morning sun glinted off his spectacles.

The buffalo was of medium size, but boasted an exceptionally long tail, which it swung vigorously from side to side as though determined to splatter its timid, inexperienced master with as much filth as possible. For all his efforts to dodge the relentless lashes, one split second of inattention was enough for Four-Eyes to receive a blow to the face from the buffalo's tail, which sent his spectacles hurtling through the air. He swore and dropped the reins from his right hand and the plough from his left. Clapping his hands over his eyes, he let out a stream of abuse as if he had been blinded.

He was so enraged that he didn't hear our jovial shouts of greeting. He was very short-sighted and was unable to distinguish us from the jeering peasants in the neighbouring paddy fields.

He bent over and plunged his arms into the water, groping around in the mud. The blank expression in his bulging eyes was disconcerting.

Four-Eyes had evidently aroused his buffalo's sadistic instinct. The creature halted, then heaved from side to side, trampling the muddy bed with vigour, as though intent upon crushing the submerged spectacles with its hooves or the lurching ploughshare.

I took off my shoes, rolled up my trousers and stepped into the paddy field, leaving Luo seated by the wayside. Four-Eyes was not eager for me to help search for his spectacles, fearing that I would be a hindrance, but in the end it was I who stepped on them inadvertently as I groped in the mud. Fortunately they were still in one piece.

His vision restored to its former clarity, Four-Eyes was shocked to see the state Luo was in.

'You look as sick as a dog!' he said.

As Four-Eyes couldn't abandon his work, he suggested we go to his place and take a rest until he returned.

He was lodged in the centre of the village. He had few

personal belongings, and was so anxious to demonstrate his complete trust in the revolutionary peasants that he never used to lock his door. The building, an old grain storehouse, was on stilts, like ours, but it had a projecting porch supported by sturdy bamboo stakes, where cereals, vegetables and spices would be spread out to dry. Luo and I settled down on the porch to enjoy the sunshine. After a time the sun slid beind a mountain peak, and there was a chill in the air. Once the sweat on Luo's body had dried, he turned ice cold. I found an old pullover belonging to Four-Eyes and draped it over his back, tying the sleeves around his neck like a scarf.

Even though the sun reappeared, he continued to complain of the cold. I went inside again to fetch a quilt from the bed, and on my way there it occurred to me that there might be another pullover lying around somewhere. I took a look under the bed, where I discovered a large wooden packing crate. Piled on top was a jumble of old shoes and broken slippers encrusted with mud and dirt.

Pulling the crate into a beam of dust-dappled sunlight, I opened it and found that it contained more articles of clothing. I was fumbling around in the hope of finding a small pullover that would fit Luo's scrawny body when my fingers suddenly came upon something soft, supple and smooth to the touch, which made me think at once of a lady's doeskin shoe.

But it was not a shoe, it was a suitcase. A ray of light bounced off the glossy lid. It was an elegant suitcase, a little worn but made of fine leather, and it gave off a whiff of civilisation.

It seemed inordinately heavy in relation to its size, but I had no way of telling what was inside. It was fastened with locks in three places.

I waited impatiently for the evening, when Four-Eyes would be released from his daily struggle with the buffalo, so that I could ask him what sort of treasure he had so securely hidden away in his secret cache.

To my surprise he didn't answer my question. All the time we were cooking he was unusually quiet, and when he did speak he took care not to mention the suitcase.

While we were eating our supper I broached the subject again. But still he said nothing.

Luo broke the silence. 'I expect they're books,' he said. 'The way you keep your suitcase locked up and hidden away is enough to betray your secret: you've got a stash of forbidden books.'

A flicker of panic showed in our short-sighted friend's eyes, then vanished behind his glasses as he composed his features into a smiling mask.

'You must be dreaming,' he said.

He reached out to touch Luo's forehead. 'Good God, such a fever! That's what's giving you these crazy ideas, it's making you delirious. Listen, we're all friends, we have some good times together, which is fine, but if you go on about such rubbish as forbidden books, dammit, then . . .'

Soon afterwards Four-Eyes bought a brass padlock from one of his neighbours, and from then on he always took the precaution of securing the door of his house with a chain.

Two weeks later the 'Broken-bowl-shards' gathered by the Little Seamstress proved effective, and Luo's malaria subsided. When he removed the bandage from his wrist he discovered a blister the size of a bird's egg, shiny and transparent. It shrank eventually until there was only a small black scar left and the bouts of fever stopped altogether. We cooked a meal at Four-Eyes's house to celebrate Luo's recovery. That night all three of us slept tightly packed in his bed. When I checked the space underneath I found that the crate was still there, but the leather suitcase had gone.

The heightened vigilance and distrust shown by Four-Eyes, in spite of the friendship between us, seemed to substantiate Luo's theory, and we grew convinced that the suitcase was indeed filled with banned books. We often discussed this between us, Luo and I, speculating wildly about the kind of books that might be among them. (At the time, no books were permitted at all, the only exceptions being those written by Mao or his cronies, and purely scientific works.) We compiled a long list of possible titles: a whole range of Chinese classics from *The Romance of the Three Kingdoms* to *The Dream of the Red Chamber* and the *Jin Ping Mei*, which was reputed to be an erotic book. Also on our list was the poetry of the Tang, Song, Ming, and Qing dynasties, and the work of traditional artists such as Zhu Da, Shi Tao, Dong Qichang . . . We even thought of including the Bible, as well as *The Words of the Five Ancients*, which had allegedly been forbidden for centuries and in which five great prophets of the Han dynasty revealed, from the summit of a sacred mountain, what the next two thousand years would bring.

Often, after extinguishing the oil lamp in our house on stilts, we would lie on our beds and smoke in the dark. Book titles poured from our lips, the mysterious and exotic names evoking unknown worlds. It was like Tibetan incense, where you need only say the name, *Zang Xiang*, to smell the subtle, refined fragrance and to see the joss sticks sweating beads of scented moisture which, in the lamplight, resemble drops of liquid gold.

'What have you heard about Western literature?' Luo asked me one day.

'Not much. You know my parents were only interested in their work. Aside from medicine they didn't know very much.'

'It was the same with mine. But one of my aunts had a few foreign books in Chinese translation. That was before the Cultural Revolution. I remember her reading to me from a book called *Don Quixote*. It was about an old knight errant, and it was a great story.'

'What happened to her books?'

'They went up in smoke. Confiscated by the Red Guards, who promptly burnt them in public, right in front of her apartment building.'

For the next few minutes we puffed on our cigarettes in the dark, despondently and without speaking. All this talk of literature was getting me down. We had been so unlucky. By the time we had finally learnt to read properly, there had been nothing left for us to read. For years the 'Western Literature' sections of the bookshops were devoted to the complete works of the Albanian Communist leader Enver Hoxha: volume after volume with gilded bindings bearing the portrait of an old man with a garish tie, impeccably groomed grey hair, and steely, hooded eyes – the left one brown, the right one slightly smaller and of a paler shade of brown turning pinkish towards the rim.

'What made you think of Western literature?' I asked Luo.

'Well, I was just wondering. That might well be what Four-Eyes has got in his leather suitcase.'

'You may be right. What with his father being a writer and his mother a poet, they must've had plenty of books at home, just as there were lots of books about Western medicine in your house and mine. But how on earth could a whole caseful have escaped the notice of the Red Guards?'

'Perhaps his parents had the sense to hide them in time.'

'They took the devil of a risk entrusting them to Four-Eyes.'

'Just as your parents and mine always dreamed that we'd be doctors like them, Four-Eyes's parents probably wanted their son to be a writer. They must have thought it would be good for him to read books, even if he had to do so in secret.'

One cold morning in early spring, snowflakes fell thick and fast for two hours, and soon the ground was blanketed with ten centimetres of fluffy snow. The village headman gave us the day off. Luo and I set out at once to visit Four-Eyes. We had heard about his stroke of bad luck: as was bound to happen, the lenses of his spectacles had been broken.

I was sure, however, that he wouldn't allow this mishap to interfere with his work, in case his myopia was taken as a sign of physical deficiency by the revolutionary peasants and they thought he was a slacker. He lived in constant terror of the peasants' opinion, for it would be up to them one day to decide whether he had been properly re-educated, and so, in theory at any rate, his future lay in their hands. In these circumstances even the slightest defect, either political or physical, could be disastrous.

Unlike us, the inhabitants of our friend's village had to carry on working in spite of the snow: great hodfuls of rice needed to be transported on foot to the district storage station, which was situated twenty kilometres away on the bank of a river whose source was in Tibet. It was time for the annual village tax contribution, and the headman had divided the total weight of rice by the number of villagers, each one being charged with carrying about sixty kilos.

We arrived to find Four-Eyes filling his hod in readiness for the journey to the rice station. We threw some snowballs at him, but he looked all round without seeing us. Without his spectacles his goggle eyes reminded me of the dull, dazed look of a Pekinese dog. He seemed quite lost and stricken, even before he had hoisted the hod of rice onto his back.

'You're mad,' Luo said to him. 'Without your glasses you won't be able to manage that mountain path.'

'I've written to my mother. She's going to send me a new pair as soon as possible, but I can't sit and do nothing until they arrive. I've got to work, that's what I'm here for. At least, that's what the headman says.'

He talked very rapidly, as if he had no time to waste on us.

'Wait,' Luo said. 'I've got an idea: we'll help you carry your hod to the rice station, and when we get back you can lend us some of those books you've got hidden in your suitcase. How's that for a deal?'

'To hell with you,' growled Four-Eyes. 'I don't know what you're talking about. I haven't got any books hidden away.'

Spluttering with anger, he hoisted the heavy burden onto his back and set off.

'Just one book will do,' Luo called after him. 'Done?'

Without replying, Four-Eyes pressed on.

The physical odds were against him. Very soon he was

embroiled in a sort of masochistic ordeal: the snow made the path more slippery than usual, and in some places he sank into it up to his ankles. He kept his bulging eyes fixed on the ground before him but couldn't see the raised stones on which he might have put his feet. He advanced blindly, tottering and lurching like a drunkard. At one point where the path fell away he extended a leg in search of a foothold, but his other leg, unable to sustain the weight of the hod on his back, buckled, and he fell to his knees. He tried to plough on in this position, without upsetting the hod on his back, scooping the snow away with his hands so as to clear a path for himself, metre by metre, until he managed to scramble to his feet again.

From afar we watched him zigzag down the path only to lose his footing again some minutes later. This time, the hod knocked against a rock as he fell, causing the contents to spill out.

We went down the path to help him collect the spilled rice. None of us spoke. I didn't dare look him in the eye. He sat back, pulled off his snow-filled boots, emptied them, and then set about warming his swollen feet by rubbing them hard between his hands.

His head kept lolling from side to side, as if it had become too heavy for his neck.

'Got a headache?' I asked him.

'No, it's my ears that are buzzing. I'll be all right.'

By the time we had finished putting all the rice back into the hod, the sleeves of my coat were encrusted with snow crystals.

'Shall we take over?' I asked Luo.

'Yes, give me a hand with the hod, will you?' he said. 'I feel cold, and some weight on my back will warm me up.'

Luo and I took turns every fifty metres or so to carry

the sixty kilos of rice. When we arrived at the storage station we were utterly exhausted.

On our return Four-Eyes gave us a book – a thin, worn volume. The author's name was Balzac.

'BA-ER-ZAR-KE'. Translated into Chinese, the name of the French author comprised four ideograms. The magic of translation! The ponderousness of the two syllables as well as the belligerent, somewhat old-fashioned ring of the name were quite gone, now that the four characters – very elegant, each composed of just a few strokes – banded together to create an unusual beauty, redolent with an exotic fragrance as sensual as the perfume wreathing a wine stored for centuries in a cellar. (Years later I learnt that the translator was himself a great writer. Having been forbidden to publish his own works for political reasons, he spent the rest of his life translating French novels.)

Did Four-Eyes stop to think about which book he would lend us? Or was it a random choice? Perhaps he picked it simply because, of all the treasures in his precious suitcase, it was the thinnest book, and the most decrepit. Did he have ulterior motives which we could not fathom? Whatever his reasons, his choice was to have a profound effect on our lives.

The slim little volume was entitled *Ursule Mirouët*.

Luo started reading the book the very same night that Four-Eyes lent it to us, and reached the end at dawn, when he put out the oil lamp and passed the book to me. I stayed in bed until nightfall, without food, completely wrapped up in the French story of love and miracles.

Picture, if you will, a boy of nineteen, still slumbering in the limbo of adolescence, having heard nothing but revolutionary blather about patriotism, Communism, ideology and propaganda all his life, falling headlong into a story of awakening desire, passion, impulsive action, love, of all the subjects that had, until then, been hidden from me.

In spite of my complete ignorance of that distant land called France (I had heard Napoleon mentioned by my father a few times, that was all), Ursule's story rang as true as if it had been about my neighbours. The messy affair over inheritance and money that befell her made the story all the more convincing, thereby enhancing the power of the words. By the end of the day I was feeling quite at home in Nemours, imagining myself posted by the smoking hearth of her parlour in the company of doctors and curates . . . Even the part about magnetism and somnambulism struck me as credible and riveting.

I did not rise from my bed until I had turned the last page. Luo had not yet returned. There had been no doubt in my mind when he set off on the mountain path at first light: he had gone to visit the Little Seamstress so he could tell her this wonderful tale of Balzac's. I stood on the threshold of our house on stilts for some time, munching a piece of corn bread as I contemplated the sombre silhouette of the mountain peak looming ahead. The village where the Little Seamstress lived was too far away for the lights in the house to be visible, but in my mind's eye I could see Luo telling her the story. Suddenly I felt a stab of jealousy, a bitter wrenching emotion I had never felt before.

It was chilly and I shivered in my short sheepskin coat. The villagers ate, slept or went about their private business in the dusk. But in front of our house on stilts everything was quiet. Usually I took advantage of the calm reigning on the mountain at this hour to practise my violin, but now it seemed a depressing thing to do. I stepped inside and picked up my instrument, but when I played it the sound was shrill and disagreeable, as if I had forgotten how to play. Then I was seized with an idea: I would copy out my favourite passages from *Ursule Mirouët*, word for word.

It was the first time in my life that I had felt any desire to copy sentences from a book. I ransacked the room for paper, but all I could find was a few sheets of notepaper intended for letters to our parents.

I decided I would write directly onto the inside of my sheepskin coat. The short coat, a gift from the villagers when I arrived, was made of skins with wool of varying lengths and textures on the outside and bare hide on the inside. It was hard to find suitable passages in the book, as the limited space afforded by my coat was further reduced by areas where the leather was too cracked to be of use. I copied out the chapter where Ursule somnambulates. I longed to be like her: to be able, while I lay asleep on my bed, to see what my mother was doing in our apartment five hundred kilometres away, to watch my parents having supper, to observe their gestures, the dishes on the table, the colour of the crockery, to sniff the aroma of their food, to hear their conversation . . . Better still, like Ursule, I would visit, in my dreams, places I had never set eyes on before . . .

Writing on the skin of an old mountain sheep was not easy: the surface was rough and creased and, in order to squeeze as much text as possible into the available space, I had to use a minute script, which required all the concentration I could muster. By the time I had covered the entire inside of the jacket, including the sleeves, my fingers were aching so badly it felt as if the bones were broken. At last I dozed off.

The sound of Luo's footsteps woke me; it was three a.m. I couldn't have been asleep for long, as the oil lamp was still alight. I saw his shadowy figure slip into the room.

'Are you asleep?'

'Not really.'

'I've got something to show you.'

He topped up the lamp with oil and, when the wick was burning brightly, he took the lamp in his left hand, came over to my bed and sat down on the edge. His eyes were blazing and his hair was rumpled. From the pocket of his jacket he drew a square of neatly folded white cloth.

'I see. The Little Seamstress has given you a handker-chief.'

He didn't reply. As he slowly unfolded the cloth, I saw that it was torn from a shirt that had undoubtedly belonged to the Little Seamstress – it had a patch sewn on by hand. Inside were some dried leaves. They all had the same pretty shape, like butterfly wings, in shades ranging from deep orange to brown streaked with pale gold, but all of them were stained black with blood.

'They're the leaves of a gingko tree,' Luo said breathlessly. 'A magnificent, towering tree that grows in a secret valley to the east of the Little Seamstress's village. We made love there, against the trunk. Standing. She was a virgin, and her blood dripped onto the leaves scattered underneath.'

Words failed me. I strained to imagine the scene: the tree, the nobility of its trunk, the grandeur of its branches, the carpet of butterfly leaves, and then I asked him: 'Standing?'

'Yes, like horses. Perhaps that's why she laughed afterwards, a laugh so piercing, so wild, and echoing so far and wide that even the birds took wing in fright.'

Once our eyes had been opened, we kept our promise and returned *Ursule Mirouët* to her rightful owner: Four-Eyes, or rather Two-Eyes now that he was bereft of his glasses. We were under the illusion that he would lend us more books from his secret suitcase, in exchange for jobs we would do for him while he was incapacitated by poor eyesight.

But he wouldn't hear of it. We often went to his house to take him food, entertain him, play the violin for him . . . Eventually the arrival of his new glasses, sent by his mother, delivered him from his semi-blindness, and put an end to our hopes for the time being.

We bitterly regretted having returned the book. 'We should never have given it back,' Luo said repeatedly. 'I could have read it out, page by page, to the Little Seamstress. That would have made her more refined, more cultured, I'm quite sure.'

It was, so he maintained, the extract copied onto the inside of my coat that had given him this idea. Luo and I were in the habit of sharing our clothes, and on one occasion – it was a day of rest – he borrowed my sheepskin coat to wear when he went to meet the Little Seamstress at the foot of their gingko tree in the valley of love. 'After I had read the passage from Balzac to her word for word,' he explained, 'she took your coat and reread the whole thing, in silence. The only sounds were the leaves rustling overhead and the faint rush of a distant waterfall. It was a beautiful day, the sky was a heavenly blue, blissful and clear. When she'd finished reading she sat there quite still, open-mouthed. Your coat was resting on the flat of her hands, the way a sacred object lies in the palms of the pious.'

'This fellow Balzac is a wizard,' he went on. 'He touched the head of this mountain girl with an invisible finger, and she was transformed, carried away in a dream. It took a while for her to come down to earth. She ended up putting your wretched coat on (which looked very good on her, I must say). She said having Balzac's words next to her skin made her feel good, and also more intelligent.'

The enthusiasm of the Little Seamstress's response made us feel even worse about having returned the book. Indeed, we had to wait until the early summer for a fresh opportunity to arise.

It was Sunday. Four-Eyes had made a fire in his yard to heat a cauldron of water which was raised up on a couple of stones. Luo and I were surprised to see him so busy around the house.

At first he didn't talk to us at all. He seemed weary and dejected. When the water boiled he took off his jacket with a look of distaste, dropped it in the cauldron and held it down with the aid of a long stick. Wreathed in thick steam, he kept stirring his miserable jacket around while little black bubbles, crumbs of tobacco and a fetid smell rose to the surface.

'Is it to kill the lice?' I asked him.

'Yes, I got covered in them on the Thousand-Metre-Cliff.'

We had heard about this cliff, but had never set foot there ourselves. It was quite far from our village, half a day's march at least.

'What were you doing there?'

He didn't reply. Methodically he stripped off his shirt, vest, trousers and socks, and plunged them in the boiling water. His thin bony body was dotted all over with angry red bumps, and the skin was broken and bleeding and covered in scratch marks.

'They're huge, the lice on that God-awful cliff. They even managed to lay their eggs in the seams of my clothes,' Four-Eyes told us.

He went into the house to fetch his underpants, which he held out to us before dropping them into the cauldron. God almighty! Lining the seams there were rows and rows of black eggs, gleaming like tiny glass beads. Just glimpsing them was enough to give me goose flesh from head to toe.

Luo and I sat side by side tending the fire, while Four-Eyes stood over the cauldron stirring the clothes with his long wooden stick. Little by little he revealed to us the secret behind his journey to the Thousand-Metre-Cliff.

Two weeks earlier he had received a letter from his mother, the poetess who had once been famous in our province for her odes on mist, rain and the blushing memory of first love. She informed him that an old friend of hers had been appointed editor-in-chief of a journal devoted to revolutionary literature, and that he had promised, despite his precarious situation, to try to find a position at the journal for her son. To avoid any semblance of favouritism, he suggested that he publish in his journal the words to a number of popular ballards, that is to say sincere, authentic folk songs full of romantic realism, which Four-Eyes would collect from the peasants on the mountain.

After receiving this news Four-Eyes walked on air. He felt completely changed. For the first time in his life he was suffused with happiness. He refused to go out to work in the fields. Instead, he threw himself heart and soul into the solitary search for mountain folk songs. He was confident that he would succeed in assembling a vast collection, which would enable his mother's former admirer to keep his promise. But a whole week passed without him coming up with a single song-line worthy of publication in an official journal.

Weeping tears of frustration, he had written to his mother telling her of his predicament. He had been on the point of handing the sealed envelope to the postman when the latter mentioned an old man who lived on the Thousand-Metre-Cliff. This old man, a poor miller, knew all the songs of the region, and although illiterate, he had the reputation of being a champion singer. Four-Eyes had torn up his letter to his mother on the spot, and had quickly set off on a fresh expedition.

'The old man's a drunkard, and he's very poor,' he told us. 'I've never seen anyone as poor in my life. D'you know what he takes with his liquor? Pebbles! I swear it's true, on the head of my mother. He dips them in salty water, puts them in his mouth, rolls them around and spits them out again. He says this dish is called "jade dumplings with miller sauce". He offered some to me, but I declined. I didn't realise I'd be hurting his feelings, but after that he became very irritated. I tried desperately to persuade him to sing for me, even offering him money, but he clammed up completely. I stayed with him at the old mill for two days in the hope of drawing him out, and I spent the night in his bed, rolled up in a quilt that can't have been washed for decades . . .'

It was not hard to imagine the scene: the bug-infested bed upon which Four-Eyes lay, fighting to stay awake in case the old man happened to sing snatches of sincere, authentic folk songs in his sleep, while the lice swarmed out of their hiding places to attack in the dark, sucking his blood, skating on the slippery lenses of his spectacles, which he hadn't removed for the night. At the slightest twitch of the old man's body, at the faintest grunt, our friend Four-Eyes would hold his breath, ready to switch on his pocket torch and take notes like a spy. But after a brief moment of suspense everything would return to normal, with the old man snoring regularly to the rhythm of the never-ending water wheel.

'I've got an idea,' Luo said casually. 'If we were to succeed in getting your miller to sing his folk songs to us, would you lend us some more books by Balzac?'

Four-Eyes didn't answer at once. He focused his steamed-up glasses on the black water bubbling in the cauldron, as though hypnotised by the dead lice somersaulting among the bubbles and tobacco flakes.

Finally he raised his head and asked Luo: 'How do you propose to go about it?'

HAD YOU seen me on my way to the Thousand-Metre-Cliff that summer's day in 1973, you would have sworn I had stepped out of an official photograph of a Communist Party conference, or out of the wedding portrait of a revolutionary cadre. I wore a navy blue jacket with a dark grey collar, made for me by the Little Seamstress. It was an exact copy of the jacket worn by Chairman Mao, from the collar down to the shape of the pockets and the trimmings on the sleeves: a trio of little brass buttons that caught the light every time I moved my arms. Seeking to disguise the youthfulness of my unruly hair, which stood out from my scalp, our wardrobe mistress had covered my head with an old green cap like an army officer's, which belonged to her father. Unfortunately, it was at least one size too small for me.

As for Luo, in keeping with his secretarial status he wore a faded army uniform, which we had borrowed the day before from a young peasant recently returned from military service. On his chest shone a fiery red badge with Mao's head in gold relief, his hair solidly slicked back.

As we had never ventured into this wild and forsaken

part of the mountain before, we very nearly lost our way in a dense forest of bamboo. The giant grasses glistening with raindrops towered all around, their tufted crowns meeting overhead and closing in on us. There was an acrid smell of invisible animals, and now and then you could hear the soft thrust of new growth and unfurling shoots. The more vigorous species of bamboo can, it seems, grow as much as thirty centimetres in a single day.

The old singer's water mill straddled a torrent that fell from a tall cliff. It was like a relic from the past, with its enormous wheels of white stone veined with black turning at an appropriately measured, rural sort of pace.

Inside, on the ground floor, the wooden planking shook. Looking down through the gaps between the ancient warped floorboards, you could see the water rushing between large rocks. The crunching sound of stone turning on stone reverberated in our ears. An old man, naked from the waist up, stood in the middle of the room, pouring grain into the milling hole. He interrupted his work when we came in and eyed us with suspicion, saying nothing. I greeted him, not in the Szechuan dialect of our province, but in Mandarin, as if I were an actor in a film.

'What language is he speaking?' the old man asked Luo, puzzled.

'The official language,' replied Luo. 'The language of Beijing. Don't you speak Mandarin?'

'Where's Beijing?'

We were taken aback by his question, but when we realised he was speaking in earnest we couldn't help laughing. For a moment I almost envied him his complete ignorance of the outside world.

'Peiping, does that ring a bell?' Luo asked.

'Bai Ping?' the old man said. 'Certainly, it's the big city in the north!'

'They changed the name twenty years ago, little father,' Luo explained. 'And this gentleman here, he speaks the official language of Bai Ping, as you call it.'

The old man threw me a look of deep respect. He stared at my Mao jacket, then fixed his eyes on the trio of buttons on the sleeves. He reached out to touch them with the tips of his fingers.

'Such pretty little things, what are they for?' he asked.

Luo translated his question for me. I replied in my shaky Mandarin that I didn't know. But my interpreter told the old miller that I had said they were the mark of a real revolutionary cadre.

'This gentleman,' Luo went on in his suave con-man voice, 'has come all the way from Beijing for the purpose of collecting the folk songs of this region, and every citizen who knows any is duty bound to pass them on to him.'

'Our mountain songs?' the old man asked, glancing suspiciously in my direction. 'They're not proper songs, you know, they're just ditties, old ditties.'

'What this gentleman is looking for is precisely that: the authentic, robustly primitive words of ancient ditties.'

The old miller mulled over this very precise request. Then he grinned at me with a strange, crafty glint in his eyes.

'Do you honestly think . . . ?'

'Yes I do,' I replied firmly.

'Does the gentleman really wish me to sing that kind of rude nonsense for him? Because, you see, our ditties, as everybody knows, are . . .'

He was interrupted by the arrival of a party of peasants carrying heavy burdens on their backs.

I was very worried indeed, as was my so-called interpreter. I whispered in his ear, 'Shall we make a run for it?' But the old man, turning to us, asked Luo: 'What's he saying?' whereupon I felt myself blush and, to hide my embarrassment, I quickly went to offer the peasants some help with unloading their burdens.

There were six of them. Not one had ever been to our village, it seemed, and once I had made sure they had no idea who we were I felt better. They deposited their heavy cargoes of maize for milling on the ground.

'Come along now, let me introduce you to this young gentleman from Bai Ping,' the old miller told the peasants. 'See the three little buttons on his sleeves?'

Transformed, radiant, the old hermit took my wrist, raised it in the air and waved it to and fro in front of the peasants for them to admire the silly yellow buttons.

'You know what they are?' he cried, liquor squirting from his mouth, 'They're the mark of a revolutionary cadre.'

I was amazed at the strength in this scrawny old man's calloused hand. His vice-like grip on my wrist almost cracked the bone. Con-man Luo stood next to us translating the miller's words into Mandarin, with all the serious air of an official interpreter. I found myself nodding and shaking hands with everyone like some political leader in a newsreel, while I stammered civilities in very poor Mandarin indeed.

Never in my life had I behaved in this way. I regretted this incognito visit, rashly undertaken to accomplish an impossible mission on behalf of Four-Eyes, cruel master of the leather suitcase.

I nodded my head so energetically that my green cap, or rather the tailor's cap, fell to the ground.

The peasants went away at long last, leaving behind a mountain of maize for grinding.

I felt utterly drained, and my head was aching badly from the tight-fitting cap, which felt more and more like a metal clamp on my skull.

The old miller led us up a shaky wooden ladder, from which two or three rungs were missing, to the next floor. There he hurried over to a rattan basket and drew out a calabash filled with liquor, and three small beakers.

'It's not so dusty here,' he said, grinning. 'Let's have a drink.'

The floor of this large, dimly lit space was scattered with pebbles, which we suspected were the 'jade dumplings' Four-Eyes had told us about. Like downstairs, there was not a stick of furniture except for a large bed. On the wall hung the dark, dappled skin of a leopard or panther and a musical instrument, a sort of bamboo viol with three strings.

The old miller invited us to sit down on his bed. It was the very bed to which Four-Eyes owed his painful memories.

I glanced at my interpreter, who was clearly just as apprehensive as I was.

'Wouldn't it be more pleasant to sit outside?' faltered Luo, his nerves beginning to fray. 'It's so dark in here.'

'Don't worry, I'll take care of that.'

The old man lit an oil lamp and put it down in the middle of the bed. The reservoir was nearly empty, so he went off in search of fuel. He returned the next minute with a calabash full of oil. He poured some into the lamp, and placed the half-full calabash next to the one containing the liquor.

Huddled around the oil lamp, we squatted on the bed

and drank. Right next to me was a bundle of soiled clothes rolled up in a spare blanket. As I sipped my drink I could feel tiny insects crawling up one of my legs. I decided to waive the protocol of my official status and slip my hand discreetly into my trousers, but immediately felt my other leg being attacked. I had a vision of my body as a rallying ground for armies of lice, all thrilled at the change of diet, ravenous for the delights offered by my poor veins. I had a vision of Four-Eyes stirring the big cauldron in which clothes billowed and sank and whirled – only it was my new Mao-style jacket seething amid the black bubbles.

After a while the old miller went away, leaving us at the mercy of the lice. He returned with a platter, a small bowl and three pairs of chopsticks, all of which he put out on the quilt next to the lamp. Then he clambered onto the bed again.

Neither Luo nor I had thought for a moment that the old man would have the gall to make us the same offer as he had made Four-Eyes. But it was too late to distract him. The platter was heaped with small, ordinary-looking pebbles in varying shades of grey and green, and the bowl contained clear water which sparkled in the light of the oil lamp. The salt crystals lying on the bottom told us that this must be the miller's sauce. Meanwhile my attackers were reaching the limits of their territorial expansion: they had got under my cap, and I could feel my hair standing on end as they raided my scalp.

'Help yourselves,' the old man told us. 'It's my usual fare: jade dumplings with salty sauce.'

He took his chopsticks, picked up a pebble from the dish and slowly dipped it in the sauce as if performing a ritual. Then he raised the pebble to his lips and sucked it with relish. He kept it in his mouth for a long time. I saw it roll around between his rotten teeth, but just as he seemed about to swallow it, it re-emerged from the depths of his throat. The old man pursed his lips and spat it out of the corner of his mouth, making it skitter across the floor.

After a moment's hesitation Luo took up his chopsticks and tasted his first jade dumpling, wearing an expression of polite approval mixed with pity. The visitor from Bai Ping, as I pretended to be, followed suit. The sauce was not too salty, and the pebble left a sour-sweet taste in my mouth.

The old man kept refilling our beakers with liquor and pressing us to join him in yet another toast. Our three mouths sent the pebbles flying through the air in an arc. Some of them struck other pebbles already strewn on the floor, making a sharp, jolly clatter.

The old man was in excellent spirits. He also had a sense of occasion. Before embarking on his mountain ditties, he went down to stop the grindstone turning, as it made too much noise. Then he went over to the window and shut it, in order to improve the acoustics. He was still naked to the waist, and he adjusted his belt of plaited straw with care before unhooking his three-stringed instrument from the wall.

'So you want to hear some old songs?' he offered.

'Indeed we do. It's for an important official journal,' Luo said in a confidential tone. 'We're counting on you, old man. What we need are sincere, authentic songs, with a touch of romantic realism.'

'What d'you mean by romantic?'

Luo pondered the question, then placed his hand on his chest, as though bearing witness before a heavenly power: 'Emotion and love.'

The old man ran his fingers lightly over the strings of his

instrument, which he held like a guitar. After a few notes he launched, almost inaudibly, into song.

Our attention was immediately drawn to the contortions of his stomach, the sight of which was so extraordinary as to obliterate his voice, the tune and everything else from our consciousness. Being so thin, he didn't actually have a stomach at all, just wrinkled skin forming innumerable tiny folds on his abdomen. When he began to sing the wrinkles billowed out, forming little waves that rippled across his tanned and gleaming body. The band of plaited straw that served as his belt began to undulate too. Every now and then it disappeared into a roll of skin, but just as it seemed lost for ever in the tidal flow it re-emerged, dignified and pristine. A magical waistband.

The old miller's voice, at once hoarse and deep, got louder and louder. While he sang his eyes flitted incessantly from Luo's face to mine and back again, his expression veering from genial complicity to a wild stare.

This is what he sang:

> *Tell me:*
> *An old louse,*
> *What does it fear?*
> *It fears boiling water,*
> *Boiling bubbling water.*
> *And the young nun,*
> *Tell me,*
> *What does she fear?*
> *She fears the old monk*
> *No more and no less*
> *Just the old monk.*

We held our sides laughing. We tried to control ourselves, of course, but the giggles inside us mounted and mounted until we exploded. The old miller smiled, too, and went on singing while the skin eddied across his stomach. Luo and I rolled over the ground in a paroxysm of hilarity.

Wiping his eyes, Luo stood up. He took the calabash and filled our three beakers while we waited for the old singer to sing the rest of this sincere, authentic, romantic mountain song.

'Let's drink to your incredible stomach,' Luo proposed.

Waving his beaker, our singer invited us to lay our hands on his abdomen. He began taking deep breaths, without singing, just for the fun of setting off the spectacular ripples across his stomach. Then we clinked our beakers and each of us gulped down the contents. For a few seconds the three of us sat there, transfixed. Then suddenly my gorge rose with a taste so vile that I forgot my role and blurted, in the broad dialect of Szechuan, 'What's your moonshine made of?'

No sooner had I asked the question than all three of us spat out what we had in our mouths, almost in unison: Luo had picked the wrong calabash. He hadn't poured us a drink of liquor, but lamp oil.

I THINK it must have been the first time since his arrival on Phoenix mountain that Four-Eyes actually beamed at anyone with deep contentment. It was hot. His face was dripping with perspiration and his glasses kept slithering down his small nose. While he pored over the pieces of paper stained with salt, liquor and lamp oil, on which we had noted down the old miller's eighteen songs, Luo and I lay sprawled on his bed, in our coats and shoes. We were dead tired: we had spent most of the night tramping across the mountain, and after crossing the bamboo forest the sounds of invisible wild animals had accompanied us from afar until dawn. Suddenly the smile faded from Four-Eyes's face, making way for a scowl.

'Bloody hell! All you've got here is a load of smutty rhymes!' he barked.

His voice had the sharp edge of an army commander. I was taken aback by his outburst, but said nothing. All we wanted was for him to lend us a couple of books in return for our exertions.

'You said you wanted authentic mountain songs,' Luo reminded him tensely.

'Ye gods! So I did, and I also told you I wanted uplifting lyrics with an undertone of romantic realism.'

As he spoke Four-Eyes held up one of the pages between finger and thumb and waved it in our faces. The crackle of paper blended with his scolding, schoolmasterly tone.

'What is it with you two, always going for stuff that's forbidden?'

'Don't exaggerate,' Luo said.

'You think I'm exaggerating? You want me to show this to the commune authorities? Your old miller would be accused of spreading erotic material. He might even go to prison. I'm serious.'

Suddenly I hated him. But I didn't show it. It was better to wait until he had kept his promise to lend us more books.

'Go on then, tell tales on the old man!' Luo said. 'I thought he was great – his songs, his voice, his weird rippling stomach, and the things he told us. I'm going back there so that I can give him some money for his kindness.'

Sitting on the edge of the bed, Four-Eyes swung his skinny legs up on the table and resumed reading our notes.

'How could you waste all that precious time writing down this drivel? I can't believe it. Do you seriously think an official journal would even consider publishing this shit? That they'd give me a job on the strength of this? You must be out of your minds.'

The change he had undergone since receiving his mother's letter was truly remarkable. A few days before it would have been unthinkable for him to snap at us like this. I hadn't suspected that a tiny glimmer of hope for the future could transform someone so utterly. He was insanely arrogant, and his voice seethed with longing and hatred. There was not the slightest mention of the books he was supposed to lend us. He jumped up, scattering our notes on the bed, and went into the kitchen. We could hear him chopping vegetables while he grumbled away.

'I suggest you collect all your papers and put them away in your pockets, or better still, burn them in the stove right away. I don't want any of that forbidden stuff lying around, least of all on my bed!'

Luo joined him in the kitchen: 'Give us a couple of books and we'll go.'

'What books?' I heard Four-Eyes whine while he went on chopping the cabbages and turnips.

'The books you promised us.'

'You think I'm crazy or what? All you've brought me is useless garbage, which will only get me into trouble! And you've got the cheek to pretend that they're . . .'

His voice stopped and he stormed into the room again, still holding his chopping knife. He grabbed the papers from the bed and ran to the window to read them over once more by the light of the early sun.

'Good God! I'm saved,' he cried. 'All I need to do is make a few alterations. I can add the right words here and there, and I can cut out the offending ones . . . Dimwits, that's what you are. At least I can think straight, which is more than I can say for the pair of you.'

Without more ado he proceeded to read out his adapted, or rather skewed, version of the first song:

Tell me:
Little bourgeois lice,
What do they fear?
They fear the boiling wave of the proletariat.

73

I leaped to my feet and lunged at him. In my indignation all I wanted was to snatch the papers from his grasp, but as I flailed my arms I involuntarily punched him on the jaw, which sent him reeling. The back of his head crashed against the wall, the knife fell from his hand, and his nose started to bleed. I tried to get hold of our notes so that I could tear them up into little bits and stuff them into his mouth, but he held on to them tight.

I hadn't been in a fight of any kind for such a long time that I got quite carried away, and for several minutes I lost track of what was happening. I noted that his mouth was wide open, but didn't hear what he was shouting.

I came to my senses again outside. Luo and I were sitting by the wayside at the foot of a boulder. Luo stabbed his finger at my Mao-style jacket, which was stained with Four-Eyes's blood.

'You look like a hero in a war movie,' he told me. 'Well, no more Balzac for the time being.'

WHENEVER ANYONE asks me what the town of Yong Jing was like I quote what my friend Luo had to say on the subject: so small that when the local canteen prepared a dish of beef and onions the smell reached the nose of every single inhabitant.

In fact, the town wasn't much more than a single high street about two hundred metres long with a post office, town hall, general store, library and school. There was also a restaurant attached to the hotel, which had a dozen rooms. At the far end of the town, halfway up a hill, was the district hospital.

That summer the headman of our village sent us to town several times to watch films. I was convinced that the real reason behind his liberal attitude was the irresistible attraction of our alarm clock, with its proud peacock-feathered rooster: our ex-opium grower turned Communist was besotted with it. The only way he could have it to all to himself, even for a short time, was to despatch us to Yong Jing. During the four days it took us to get there, see the film and return to our village, he would be lord and master of the clock.

Towards the end of August, that is to say one month after our argument with Four-Eyes and the ensuing breakdown in diplomatic relations, we set off for Yong Jing again, but this time we were accompanied by the Little Seamstress.

The basketball court turned open-air cinema was crammed with spectators. They were still showing the old North Korean film *The Little Flower Seller*, which had moved the four sorceresses in the Little Seamstress's house to tears. It was a bad film, and seeing it a second time was not likely to change our opinion. But that didn't dampen our spirits. For one thing, we were glad to be in town again, even a town no bigger than a pocket handkerchief. Memories of city life came flooding back and, believe me, even the smell of beef and onions savoured of sophistication. What is more, Yong Jing had electricity instead of the oil lamps we were used to. I wouldn't go so far as to say that our visits to town had become an obsession, but at least having to trudge across the mountain to see a film meant getting four days off from labouring in the fields, from carrying human and animal dung on our backs, or from toiling in the paddy fields with water buffalo whose long tails whacked you across the face.

The other reason for our high spirits was that the Little Seamstress was with us. By the time we arrived the film had already started, and there was only standing room left behind the screen, where everything was in reverse and everyone was left-handed. But the Little Seamstress didn't want to miss this rare treat. As for us, we were content to watch her lovely face bathed in the luminous colours bouncing off the screen. Now and then everything would go dark and her eyes would shine like spots of phosphorous in the gloom. Then suddenly, when the scene changed, her face would light up, flush with colour, and blossom with wonder. Of all the girls in the audience, and there were at least two thousand, she was certainly the prettiest. A sense of masculine pride stirred deep inside us, surrounded as we were by the jealous looks of the other men in the crowd. About halfway into the film, she turned to me and whispered in my ear. Her words pierced my heart.

'It's so much better when it's you telling the story.'

The hotel we went to afterwards was very cheap – five pence for a room, barely the price of a portion of beef and onions. In the courtyard we came upon the old bald-headed night watchman, whom we already knew, dozing on a chair. He pointed up at one of the windows where a light was shining, and told us in a low voice that the room had been taken for the night by a woman travelling on her own. She was aged about forty, he said, and had come from the provincial capital. She would be leaving for Phoenix mountain in the morning.

'It's her son she has come for,' he added. 'She has found him a good job in the city.'

'Her son's being re-educated?' Luo asked.

'Yes, just like you.'

Who could this fortunate person be – the first of the hundred-odd city youths on our mountain to be released from re-education? The question kept us awake at least half the night, feverish with envy. Our beds felt as if they were on fire, it was impossible to sleep in them. We had no idea who the lucky boy might be, although we went over and over the names of everyone we thought might be a candidate, excluding those of us who belonged in the three-in-a-thousand category because we were sons of

77

bourgeois parents, like Four-Eyes, or sons of class enemies, like Luo and me.

We were on our way home the next day when I happened to meet the woman who had come to rescue her son. Just before the footpath rose steeply among the rocks to lose itself in the white clouds shrouding the peaks, we caught sight of a vast slope dotted with Tibetan and Chinese tombs. The Little Seamstress wanted to show us where her maternal grandfather was buried. Not being partial to cemeteries myself, I stayed behind while she and Luo explored the forest of tombstones, some of which were half submerged in the ground, others covered in thick creeper.

I settled down under an overhanging rock and, as usual, lit a fire with dry leaves and some branches. I took a couple of sweet potatoes out of my bag, and was burying them among the embers when I looked up to see the woman sitting in a wooden chair lashed to the shoulders of a young man. What was really surprising was that, in her none too steady seat, she displayed an almost superhuman serenity and was knitting, as though she were sitting on her balcony at home.

A slight figure, she wore a dark green cord jacket, tan trousers and a pair of flat-soled shoes made of soft greenish leather. When they drew abreast with me, her porter decided to have a rest and lowered the chair onto a flat-topped rock. The woman simply went on knitting, making no move to get down from her chair. She didn't even glance at what I was doing, nor did she exchange a single word with her porter. Using the local accent, I asked her if she had spent the night at the hotel in Yong Jing. She nodded her head in confirmation and resumed her knitting. She was an elegant and, undoubtedly, rich woman who wasn't going to be taken aback by anything.

I took a stick and speared a sweet potato from among the smoking embers, tapping it against a stone a few times to shake off the ash. I decided to switch to another accent.

'May I offer you a taste of mountain roast?'

'You speak with a Chengdu accent!' she exclaimed. Her voice was gentle and melodic.

I explained that Chengdu was where my relatives lived, that it was my home town. At this she got out of her chair and, still holding her knitting, came over to sit by my fire. She was clearly not used to squatting down in such informal circumstances.

She accepted my offer of the sweet potato with a smile and blew on it, but avoided taking a bite by asking what had brought me to this remote place. Was I being re-educated?

'Yes, on Phoenix mountain,' I replied, poking my stick into the ashes to find another sweet potato.

'Really?' she cried. 'That's where my son is being re-educated. You may have met him. It seems he's the only one up there who wears glasses.'

The point of my stick glanced off the sweet potato, stabbing the ashes. My head swam, as if I had been struck in the face.

'Is your son Four-Eyes?'

'Yes he is.'

'So he's the first of us to be released!'

'Oh, have you heard? Yes indeed, he is going to work for a literary journal.'

'Your son's an incredible expert on folk songs.'

'I know. At first we were afraid he'd be wasting his time on the mountain. But we were mistaken. He has

79

assembled a collection of splendid peasant songs, which he has adapted and modified. The editor-in-chief has shown great interest in the words.'

'It's thanks to you that he was able to do his research. You gave him plenty of books to read.'

'Of course.'

She lapsed into silence, then glared at me with suspicion.

'Books? Certainly not,' she said coldly. 'Thank you very much for the potato.'

She was truly perturbed. Seeing her discreetly replace her sweet potato among the embers, rise to her feet and make ready to continue her journey, I regretted having raised the subject of books.

Suddenly she spun round and asked me the question I had been dreading: 'What's your name? I'd like to be able to tell my son whom I met on the way.'

'My name?' I echoed warily. 'My name's Luo.'

Hardly had this lie escaped me when I was filled with remorse. I can still hear the emotion in that gentle melodic voice as Four-Eyes's mother cried out: 'So you must be the son of the great dentist! What a surprise! Is it true what they say about your father treating Chairman Mao's teeth?'

'Who told you that?'

'My son told me, in one of his letters.'

'I didn't know.'

'Didn't your father tell you? How very modest of him! He is reputed to be a very great dentist, very great.'

'Actually, he's in detention at the moment. He's been classed as an enemy of the people.'

'So I've heard. Four-Eyes's father has been having similar problems.' Her voice sank to a whisper. 'But I shouldn't let it worry you too much. Right now, ignorance is in fashion, but one day the need for good doctors will be recognised once more. Besides, Chairman Mao is bound to need your father's services again.'

'The next time I see my father I will certainly pass on your sympathy to him.'

'You shouldn't lose hope either. As for me, although I seem to be busy knitting this blue jumper, what I'm really doing is composing poems in my head, while my hands are occupied.'

'How fascinating!' I said. 'What sort of poems are they, may I ask?'

'That is confidential, dear boy.'

With the point of one of her knitting needles she speared a sweet potato, which she skinned and then popped, piping hot, into her mouth.

'My son likes you very much, did you know? He has mentioned you many times in his letters.'

'Really?'

'Yes. But he's not so fond of your friend, it seems: the young man living in the same village as you.'

Quite a revelation. I congratuated myself on having assumed Luo's identity.

'Why doesn't he like him?' I asked, trying to sound casual.

'I think he's a bit sly. He suspects my son of having a suitcase hidden away, and every time he comes to visit he is constantly looking for it.'

'A suitcase full of books?'

'I wouldn't know,' she said, suspicious again. 'One day my son got so angry with the fellow that he punched him on the jaw and gave him a beating. I'm told he bled profusely.'

I spluttered with indignation, and had to quell the urge

to tell her that her son's vivid imagination was better suited to fiction than to faking folk songs.

'I didn't know my son was so strong,' she went on. 'In my next letter I warned him to stay out of trouble and never to get involved in such a dangerous situation again.'

'My friend will be very disappointed to hear that your son is leaving us for good.'

'Why? Did he want to get his own back?'

'No, I don't think so. But he'll have to give up hope of ever laying hands on the secret suitcase.'

'Well, that's too bad, I'm sure.'

As her porter was beginning to show impatience, she bade me goodbye. Wishing me luck, she settled herself in her chair, took up her knitting, and was gone.

The tomb belonging to the Little Seamstress's ancestor was some distance from the main footpath; it stood on a south-facing corner of the slope among the graves of the poor. Some were little more than mounds of earth, of varying sizes. Others were in slightly better condition, their headstones sinking into the tall, wilting grass. The ancestor's grave was very modest, insignficant even. It was marked with a dark grey stone veined with blue, eroded by decades of harsh weather, and inscribed with just one name and two dates encapsulating an unremarkable life. Luo and the Little Seamstress laid down bunches of wild flowers they had picked nearby: redbud blooms with heart-shaped, enamelled leaves, cyclamens on elegantly curved stems, balsam flowers known locally as 'Phoenix fairies', and also some rare wild orchids with immaculate milk-white petals set around a heart of the softest yellow.

'Why the long face?' the Little Seamstress called out to me.

'I'm grieving for Balzac,' I shouted back.

I went down the slope to join them and told them about my encounter with Four-Eyes's mother, the knitting poetess. They didn't seem to share my indignation at the scandalous theft of the old miller's songs, nor were they unduly affected by the news that Four-Eyes would be leaving the mountain, nor indeed by the prospect of losing Balzac. But they were greatly amused when I told them I had pretended to be Luo, the dentist's son, and their laughter filled the silence of the graveyard.

Once again, I watched the Little Seamstress's face with fascination. She was breathtaking, as she had been the night before at the open-air cinema. But now that she was laughing I was so utterly captivated that I wanted to marry her there and then, regardless of her being Luo's girlfriend. In her peals of laughter I caught the musky fragrance of wild orchids, stronger than the scent of the flowers lying at her feet.

Luo and I remained standing while she knelt down by her grandfather's grave. She prostrated herself several times, speaking soothing words to him in a kind of murmured monologue.

Suddenly she swung her head round to face us.

'About those books of his — what if we stole them?'

IT WAS thanks to the Little Seamstress that we were able to keep track, almost by the hour, of everything that went on in Four-Eyes's village during the week preceding his departure, which was planned for September 4th. All the local gossip reached her ears. She had merely to listen to the patter of her customers, among whom there were men and women, headmen and children from all the villages in the area. Nothing escaped her.

Four-Eyes and his mother the poetess were planning a grand celebration to mark the end of his stint of re-education. Rumour had it that the poetess had bribed the village headman into giving his approval for a farewell banquet to be held in the open air. The event, which would be attended by all the villagers, called for the slaughter of a buffalo.

There was some confusion about which buffalo would be killed and in what manner, because it was against the law to slaughter working animals that were used in the fields.

Although we were the only two friends Four-Eyes ever made on the mountain, we were not on the guest list – not that we minded. Indeed, the banquet would provide an excellent opportunity for us to carry out our plan to steal the secret suitcase.

The Little Seamstress had a chest that had been part of her mother's dowry, and in the bottom of one of the drawers Luo found a few large rusty nails. Like a pair of expert burglars we set about fashioning a master-key out of one of the old nails. We were so elated! I rubbed the nail against a rock until it became too hot to handle, after which I wiped it on my mud-encrusted trousers and polished it vigorously until the metal shone like new. When I held it up for inspection it sparkled so brightly I thought I could see my eyes and the late summer sky reflected in it. Luo took charge of the most delicate stage: holding the nail down on the stone with one hand, he raised the hammer with the other and swung it. The hammer head described a handsome curve in the air as it came down on the piece of metal, rebounding on impact in readiness for the next swing, and the next, until at last the required flatness had been obtained.

One or two days before the break-in, I dreamed that Luo had entrusted the master-key to me. There was a lot of mist, and I approached Four-Eyes's house stealthily, almost on tiptoe. Luo was on the lookout under a tree. We could hear the villagers shouting and singing revolutionary songs as they feasted nearby. The entrance to Four-Eyes's house had a double door. Each side was hinged in two holes, one in the threshold, the other in the lintel, and they were secured in the middle with a chain and a copper padlock. The lock was cold and beaded with moisture, and resisted my attempts to pick it for a long time. I turned the master-key this way and that, and twisted it round with such force that I was afraid it would snap off in the keyhole. Finally I grabbed hold of the left door and tried with all my might to wrench it free from the lower pivot hole. I didn't succeed. As a last resort I tried the master-key again, and suddenly, with a dry click, the padlock gave way. I pushed open the double doors, but hardly had I stepped inside when I froze in horror: there, perched on a chair behind a table was Four-Eyes's mother, calmly knitting. She smiled, without speaking. I felt myself blushing and my ears turning red-hot, like a teenager on his first romantic assignation. She didn't seem in the least alarmed. I stammered something about a message for her son, to find out where he was. She went on smiling, but didn't reply. The knitting needles flew in her long bony fingers, and I noticed she had liver spots on the backs of her hands. I was mesmerised by the clicking needles twisting and turning at breakneck speed – in, round, through, off – to knit row upon row of stitches. I retraced my steps, slipped outside, shut the two halves of the door quietly behind me, and replaced the padlock. Although there was not a sound from the house, I turned and fled as if my life depended on it. It was at that point that I woke up with a start.

For all his assertions that first-time burglars had luck on their side, Luo was just as anxious as I was. He thought about my dream for a long while, and ended up making some slight adjustments to the plan.

Towards noon on September 3rd, the day before Four-Eyes and his mother were to leave, we heard the frantic bellowing of a buffalo in agony rising up from the bottom of a ravine. The sound reverberated against the cliff and the echo reached the Little Seamstress's house. A few minutes later a bunch of children came running with the news that the headman of Four-Eyes's village had deliberately pushed a buffalo over a precipice.

The slaughter was disguised as an accident; the perpetrator claimed that the beast had lost its footing on a tight bend and had plunged head first down the cliff. Its fall had been broken by a huge jutting rock, from which the mangled body slid only to land with a dull thud on another rock a dozen metres further down.

The buffalo was still alive. I will never forget how affected I was by its long drawn-out, plaintive bellows. Under normal circumstances the bellow of a buffalo is disagreeably harsh, but on this calm late summer's day the sound echoing through the rocky mountains was imposing and sonorous, like the roaring of a lion in a cage.

A few hours later Luo and I went to the scene of the accident. The buffalo's lowing had subsided. We elbowed our way through the crowd gathered at the edge of the ravine. Apparently word had come from the commune leader that the animal could be put out of its misery. Relieved at having received sanction from on high, the headman, accompanied by Four-Eyes and half a dozen villagers, had clambered down to the bottom of the cliff to cut the animal's throat.

By the time we arrived the deed had been done. Down in the bottom of the ravine, where the execution had taken place, we spotted Four-Eyes crouching by the inert mass of the dead buffalo: he was collecting the blood pouring from the gash in a big upturned hat woven of bamboo leaves.

The six villagers launched into song and started climbing back up the steep cliff, carrying the carcass between them. Four-Eyes and his headman stayed down below. They sat side by side, hunched over the bamboo-leaf hat filled with buffalo blood.

'What are they doing down there?' I asked the man standing next to me.

'They're waiting for the blood to congeal,' he replied. 'It's a remedy against cowardice. To gain courage, you must swallow it when it's still lukewarm and frothy.'

Luo, who was curious by nature, suggested going down part of the way to get a closer look. Four-Eyes glanced up at the crowd from time to time, but it was impossible to say whether he had noticed our presence among the onlookers. At long last the headman took out his knife, which had a surprisingly long, pointed blade. He caressed the edge with the tips of his fingers and then sliced the pudding of thick blood in two: half for Four-Eyes, half for himself.

The poetess was nowhere to be seen. What would she have thought if she had been there with us to watch her son bury his face in his cupped hands and slurp the clotted buffalo blood, like a swine rooting in the mire? When he had finished he sucked his fingers one by one, to make sure not a drop was wasted. As he made his way up the steep incline I noted he was still smacking his lips to prolong the taste.

'Just as well the Little Seamstress didn't come with us,' Luo said.

Night fell. Columns of smoke rose from Four-Eyes's village; in a clearing a huge cauldron was on the boil. The receptacle was truly enormous, and must have been a village heirloom.

From our vantage point the scene made a pastoral, good-natured impression. We were too far away to see the chunks of buffalo meat bubbling in the big cauldron, but the powerful smell – spicy and a trifle coarse – made our mouths water. The villagers were gathered around the fire with the women and children in front. Some people had brought potatoes, which they dropped into the cauldron, others had come with logs and branches to feed the flames. Little by little further ingredients were added to the stew: eggs, maize cobs, dried fruit. Four-Eyes's mother was the undisputed star of the evening. She was a fine-looking woman in her own way. She wore a flower pinned to her breast – perhaps it was a gillyflower. Her glowing complexion, heightened by the green of her cord jacket, made a singular contrast with the dark, tanned faces of the mountain folk. She showed her knitting to the women, and her handiwork, although unfinished, elicited cries of admiration all round.

The appetising aroma wafting towards us in the evening air became more and more penetrating. The slaughtered buffalo must have been extremely old, because its stringy flesh took longer to cook than that of a superannuated eagle. To us prospective thieves, the delay was harrowing, but Four-Eyes, a fresh convert to blood-drinking, was no less frustrated: we saw him jumping up and down with excitement, raising the lid of the cauldron, dipping his chopsticks into the stew, taking out a lump of steaming meat, sniffing it, inspecting it closely, and dropping it back with a disappointed shrug.

We were huddled together in the shadows behind a rock. Luo murmured in my ear, pointing his finger.

'Look! Here come the guests of honour!'

The new arrivals were five old, withered crones. They wore long black robes which flapped in the autumn wind. In spite of the distance between them and us, I could make out their faces, which were as alike as sisters. Their features seemed carved in wood, and I recognised among them the four sorceresses who had come to the vigil at the Little Seamstress's house.

They had apparently been invited to the farewell banquet at the instigation of the poetess. There was a brief discussion, which ended when she took some bank notes out of her purse and gave one to each, under the covetous eyes of the villagers.

This time there was not just the one sorceress with a bow and arrow – all five of them were so armed. Who knows, maybe a bigger array of weapons was required to secure the safe passage of one privileged individual than to protect the soul of a man stricken with malaria. On the other hand, the Little Seamstress may have been unable to afford as much as the poetess, whose name was once celebrated throughout this province with its population of one hundred million.

While they were all waiting for the buffalo meat to have stewed long enough to be tender, one of the old women took Four-Eyes's left hand and read his palm in the light of the blazing fire.

We were just out of earshot and couldn't catch what the sorceress was saying, but we had a good view of her lowered eyelids, thin pinched lips and toothless gums as she muttered away. Four-Eyes and his mother listened spellbound. When she stopped talking, everyone stared at her. An uneasy silence ensued, until all the villagers started talking at once.

'I expect she made some gloomy prediction,' Luo said.

'Such as: his precious suitcase is about to be stolen.'

'No, I bet it was something about demons getting in his way.'

And he was probably right, because the next thing we saw was all five sorceresses rising up, swinging their bows belligerently into the air and crossing them with their arrows while they uttered piercing cries.

Then they performed a dance of exorcism around the fire. They started off at a slow pace, no doubt because of their great age, wheeling round and round on the spot, eyes fixed on the ground. From time to time they raised their heads and glanced anxiously around before bowing them again and intoning, like Buddhist monks, unintelligible incantations that were taken up by the crowd. Suddenly two of the sorceresses threw down their arms and started shaking all over, presumably to signal the presence of demons. It certainly looked as if their bodies had been invaded by spirits, for the spasms made horrible monsters of them. The remaining three sorceresses arched their bows and pretended to let fly at their shaking sisters, making exaggerated imitations of the sound of arrows whizzing through the air. They resembled three ravens. As they danced their long black robes billowed in the smoke then dropped to the ground, raising little clouds of dust.

The movements of the two dancing demons grew heavy, as if the invisible arrows had been tipped with poison, and after a while they slowed to a halt. Luo and I left just before their undoubtedly spectacular collapse onto the ground.

The banquet was about to begin. We heard the chanting reach its climax as we flitted across the village.

Since there was not a single villager, young or old, who hadn't jumped at the chance of some tasty buffalo meat stewed with cloves and chopped peppers, the place was deserted, exactly as foreseen by my friend Luo (who had revealed a gift for strategy as well as for narrative). Suddenly my dream came back to me.

'Shall I keep a lookout?' I asked him.

'No,' he said. 'We're not in your dream.'

Luo took the rusty nail now transformed into a master-key and moistened it between his lips. The key slid noiselessly into place, turned to the left, then the right, left again and a fraction the other way . . . there was a dry metallic click, and the copper padlock yielded at last.

We slipped into Four-Eyes's house, and immediately shut the double doors behind us. The place was so dark we could barely distinguish each other's faces. But there was a sense of imminent departure in the air, which made us ache with envy.

I peered out through the slit between the doors: there was not a soul to be seen. To be on the safe side – that is, to make sure no busybody happening to pass by would notice the padlock was missing – we pushed the doors far enough out to enable Lou, as planned, to slip one hand through, replace the chain and fasten the padlock.

When Luo switched on his torch we momentarily forgot all our carefully laid plans and stared in awe, for right there, on top of the stack of luggage, was the soft leather suitcase, glowing in the dark as though clamouring to reveal its contents.

'There it is!' I cried.

When planning our strategy a few days earlier we had come to the conclusion that the success of our illegal entry hinged on one thing: knowing where Four-Eyes had hidden his suitcase. How would we find it? Luo had pondered every conceivable solution, and in the end, thank God, he had come up with a plan. It had to be carried out during the farewell banquet. It was a unique opportunity: the poetess was no fool, of course, but she had reached the age at which being well organised becomes all-important. Little could be worse on the morning of her departure than a last-minute rush to get the suitcase from wherever it was hidden:

everything would have to be ready in advance, and in impeccable order.

We crept up to the suitcase. It was tied with a thick rope of plaited straw, knotted crosswise. We removed the rope and raised the lid in silence. Inside, piles of books shone in the light of our torch: a company of great Western writers welcomed us with open arms. On top was our old friend Balzac, with five or six novels, then came Victor Hugo, Stendhal, Dumas, Flaubert, Baudelaire, Romain Rolland, Rousseau, Tolstoy, Gogol, Dostoevsky, and some English writers, too: Dickens, Kipling, Emily Brontë . . .

We were beside ourselves. My head reeled, as if I'd had too much to drink. I took the novels out of the suitcase one by one, opened them, studied the portraits of the authors, and passed them on to Luo. Brushing them with the tips of my fingers made me feel as if my pale hands were in touch with human lives.

'It reminds me of a scene in a film,' said Luo. 'You know, when a stolen suitcase turns out to be stuffed with money . . .'

'So, are you weeping tears of joy?' I said.

'No. All I feel is loathing.'

'Me too. Loathing for everyone who kept these books from us.'

Hearing myself utter this last sentence frightened me, as if there might be an eavesdropper hidden somewhere in the room. Such a remark, casually dropped, could cost several years in prison.

'Let's go!' Luo said, shutting the suitcase.

'Wait!'

'What's the matter?'

'I'm not sure . . . Let's have another think: Four-Eyes is

bound to suspect us when he finds his suitcase gone. If he denounces us we'll be finished. Our parents aren't like the others, remember.'

'I told you before, his mother would never allow it, or the whole world would find out that her son's been harbouring forbidden books. And that would ruin his chances of leaving the Phoenix of the Sky.'

After a few moments' silence I reopened the suitcase: 'What if we just take a few? He won't notice.'

'But I want to read all of them,' Luo said resolutely.

He shut the suitcase again and, resting one hand on the lid like a Christian taking a solemn oath, he declared: 'With these books I shall transform the Little Seamstress. She'll never be a simple mountain girl again.'

We moved stealthily towards the adjoining room. I went first with the torch, and Luo followed behind carrying the suitcase. It seemed to be very heavy, for as we made our way I could hear it bang against Luo's legs and bump into Four-Eyes's bed and his mother's makeshift bunk made of wooden planks, which although small made the space seem even more cramped.

We were startled to find the window, through which we had planned to make our getaway, secured with a nail. In our excitement at seeing the suitcase, we had forgotten to check it when we arrived. We tried pushing, but all we heard was a faint creak, almost a sigh. It wouldn't budge.

. The situation didn't strike us as disastrous. We returned quietly to the main room intending to carry out the same manoeuvre as before: widening the slit in the double door just enough to allow a hand to slip through and turn the master-key in the copper padlock.

Suddenly Luo whispered: 'Shush!'

Terrified, I immediately switched the torch off. The soft

padding of feet outside held us transfixed. It took us a precious minute to realise that the footsteps were indeed coming in our direction.

At that moment we heard the muffled voices of a man and a woman, but couldn't make out whether or not they belonged to Four-Eyes and his mother. Preparing for the worst, we crept towards the kitchen. In passing the pile of luggage I switched the torch on for a second while Luo replaced the suitcase.

It was exactly as we feared: Four-Eyes and his mother were upon us and would catch us red-handed. They were talking by the door.

'I'm sure it's the buffalo blood that has upset me,' the son said. 'I keep having these evil-smelling burps.'

'Just as well I brought some medicine for indigestion,' retorted his mother.

Panic-stricken, we were at a loss for somewhere to hide in the kitchen. It was pitch dark. I collided with Luo just as he was raising the lid of a container for storing rice. He was at his wits' end.

'Too small,' he whispered.

The chain rattled and we just had time to bolt into the side room and crawl under the beds before the door flew open.

They stepped into the house and lit the oil lamp.

Things were not looking good. Instead of hiding under Four-Eyes's bed, which would have made sense as I was taller and heftier than Luo, I was stuck under his mother's bed in a very tight space which, judging by the unmistakable odour, I was sharing with a soil bucket. Flies swarmed around my head. Making as little noise as possible I tried to lie down flat but bumped against the nauseating bucket, almost spilling the contents; I heard a little splash, which only made the horrible stench worse. I jerked my head in a reflex action, thereby inadvertently making a sound loud enough to be noticed, and so give us away.

'Did you hear something, Ma?' we heard Four-Eyes ask.

'No.'

A complete hush descended, which seemed to last for ever. I pictured the two of them frozen in dramatic poses while they strained their ears to catch the slightest noise.

'All I can hear is your stomach rumbling,' the poetess declared.

'It's the buffalo blood. I feel really bad, I don't know if I can make it back to the feast.'

'I'm not having any of that! We must go back,' the mother insisted in an authoritarian voice. 'There, I've found the tablets. You'd better take two, that'll take care of your stomach ache.'

I could hear Four-Eyes heading dutifully to the kitchen, no doubt to get some water. The light of the oil lamp receded with him. Although I couldn't see Luo in the dark, I knew he was just as relieved as I was that we hadn't hidden in the kitchen.

After swallowing his tablets Four-Eyes returned to the main room. His mother asked him if he was sure he had tied the rope around the suitcase with the books.

'Of course I am. I did it earlier on.'

'But look! Can't you see the rope lying on the floor?'

How stupid of us to have opened the suitcase! A shiver ran down my spine as I crouched under the bed. I cursed myself for taking such a risk. In the gloom I tried in vain to catch the eye of my accomplice.

Four-Eyes spoke calmly, but his voice betrayed his unease: 'I dug up the suitcase behind the house as soon as it was dark. When I came inside I wiped off all the soil and filth and checked carefully to see whether the damp had got to the books. Before leaving home to join the feast, I tied it up with this straw rope.'

'So what happened? Can someone have got into the house while we were out?'

Holding the lamp in his hand, Four-Eyes crossed towards the side room. Under the other bed I could see Luo's eyes flash in the approaching light. Thank goodness Four-Eyes halted in the doorway. Turning round he declared to his mother: 'It's impossible. The window's still nailed fast and the door was padlocked when we got here.'

'Still, I think you'd better look in the suitcase to make sure there aren't any books missing. Those two friends of yours worry me. I told you in my letters I don't know how many times not to get involved with such types, they're too sly for you, but you wouldn't listen.'

I heard the lid being raised and Four-Eyes replying to his mother's complaint: 'I stayed friends with them because I thought you and Pa had problems with your teeth, and that one day Luo's father might be of assistance.'

'Really?'

'Yes, Ma.'

'You are a darling, my son.' (The mother's voice waxed sentimental.) 'Even in such difficult circumstances you still think of your parents' welfare.'

'Ma, I've checked: there's not a single book missing.'

'Just as well, it must have been a false alarm. Come on, let's go.'

'Wait, pass me the buffalo tail will you, I want to put it in the suitcase.'

A few minutes later, while he was making a knot in the rope, I heard Four-Eyes exclaim: 'Shit!'

'Mind your language now, my son.'

'I've got the runs,' Four-Eyes wailed.

'Use the bucket in the bedroom!'

To our immense relief we heard Four-Eyes running out of the house.

'Where are you off to?' the mother cried.

'To the maize field.'

'Have you got some paper?'

'No,' replied the son from afar.

'I'll get you some!' the mother called.

What luck that this would-be poet preferred to relieve his bowels in the open air! I can just see the horrific, stomach-churning scene that would have been inflicted on us had he chosen to pull the bucket out from under the bed and expel the buffalo blood in a horrible stream, or rather torrent, under our very noses.

No sooner had the mother run out of the house than I heard Luo murmuring in the dark: 'Quick, let's get out of here!'

Luo swept the suitcase off the pile of luggage as he made for the door. It was only after an hour's headlong flight along the mountain path that we finally dared stop. Luo opened the suitcase. On top of the neatly stacked books lay the buffalo tail: black with a tufted end, and stained with dark blood.

It was exceptionally long, and no doubt once belonged to the unfortunate buffalo responsible for breaking Four-Eyes's glasses.

PART III

IT WAS all such a long time ago, but one particular image from our stint of re-education is still etched in my memory with extraordinary precision: a red-beaked raven keeping watch as Luo crawled along a narrow track with a yawning chasm on either side. On his back he carried the inconspicuous, work-soiled bamboo hod in which he had secreted *Old Go*, as Balzac's *Père Goriot* was titled in Chinese – the book he was going to read to the Little Seamstress, the lovely mountain girl in need of culture.

During the whole month of September following our successful burglary we were seduced, overwhelmed, spellbound by the mystery of the outside world, especially the world of women, love and sex as revealed to us by these Western writers day after day, page after page, book after book. Not only had Four-Eyes left the mountain without daring to denounce us, also, as luck would have it, our headman had gone away to the town of Yong Jing to attend a Communist Party conference. In the ensuing political vacuum our village lapsed into quiet anarchy, and Luo and I stopped going to work in the fields without the villagers – themselves unwilling converts from opium farmers to guardians of our souls — raising the slightest objection. I kept my door more securely locked than ever and passed the time with foreign novels. Since Balzac was Luo's favourite I put him to one side, and with the ardour and earnestness of my eighteen years I fell in love with one author after another: Flaubert, Gogol, Melville, and even Romain Rolland.

Let me tell you about Romain Rolland. Among the books in Four-Eyes's suitcase there was only one by him: volume one of his four-volume masterpiece, *Jean-Christophe*. The Chinese translation was by Fu Lei, who also did the Balzac translations. As the story was about a musician and I myself played pieces on the violin such as *Mozart is Thinking of Chairman Mao*, I was naturally drawn to the book. I had intended only a brief flirtation, a skim read, but once I had opened the book I couldn't put it down. Until then short stories had been my favourite reading: well wrought and sparkling with ideas, tales that made you laugh or took your breath away, that would stay with you for the rest of your days. I was more dubious about full-length novels. But Jean-Christophe, with his fierce individualism utterly untainted by malice, was a salutary revelation. Without him I would never have understood the splendour of taking free and independent action as an individual. Up until this stolen encounter with Romain Rolland's hero, my poor educated and re-educated brains had been incapable of grasping the notion of one man standing up against the whole world. The flirtation turned into a grand passion. Even the excessively emphatic style occasionally indulged in by the author did not detract from the beauty of this astonishing work of art. I was carried away, swept along by the mighty stream of words pouring from the hundreds of pages. To me it was the ultimate book: once you had read it, neither your own life nor the world you lived in would ever look the same.

My passion for *Jean-Christophe* was so great that, for the first time in my life, I wanted something to be my very own rather than a possession I shared with Luo. So I wrote an inscription on the flyleaf to the effect that the book was a gift for my next birthday, and asked Luo to sign it. He said he was flattered, as the occasion was so momentous that it deserved to go down in history. He calligraphed his name with a single brushstroke, unbridled, lavish, spirited, linking together the three characters with an elegant flourish that took up almost half the page. For my part, I dedicated three books by Balzac to him as a gift for the coming New Year: *Père Goriot*, *Eugénie Grandet* and *Ursule Mirouët*. Beneath my dedication I drew three figures representing the three Chinese characters constituting my name. The first was a galloping horse with a long mane flying in the wind, the second a long pointed sword with a finely carved bone handle set with diamonds, and the third was a bell, around which I drew a number of short strokes like rays to suggest that it was sounding the alarm. I was so pleased with my dedication that I was tempted to add a drop or two of my blood, by way of consecration.

Towards the middle of the month, a violent storm raged on the mountain. It lasted all night long; the rain was torrential. The next morning Luo, true to his ambition to endow the lovely Little Seamstress with culture, set off at first light with *Père Goriot* in his bamboo hod. Like a knight errant, though lacking a steed, he vanished into the morning mist shrouding the path to the Little Seamstress's village.

Not wishing to break the curfew imposed by the political authority, he retraced his steps in the evening and returned meekly to our house on stilts. He said the rain had created havoc on the mountain, and that he had been obliged to climb a vertiginous, narrow ridge thrown up by an enormous landslide.

'The Little Seamstress and you would have run right over it,' he said dolefully. 'But I had to get down on my hands and knees and crawl, I was that scared.'

'Was it a long way?'

'At least forty metres.'

It was a mystery to me why Luo, who seemed so daring in all things, should have such a dread of heights. He was an intellectual type, and had never climbed a tree in his life. I still remember the afternoon in our boyhood when we were seized with the idea of climbing the rusty iron ladder of a water tower. Right from the start he scraped the palms of his hands on the rust, and when we were fifteen metres up he said, 'I keep having the feeling the rungs will collapse under my weight.' His hands were bleeding and painful, which only increased his fear. In the end he gave up, leaving me to climb the rest of the way on my own; from the top of the tower I leaned over to spit down on him for a joke, but my spittle was swept away by the wind. Five or six years had passed since then, but his dread of heights had not diminished. And he was quite right about the Little Seamstress and me having no trouble at all running over the narrowest mountain ridge. In fact, once we had reached the other side we would often have to wait for Luo to catch up with us, which could take a long time because he had to get down and crawl.

One day, for a change of air, I decided to accompany Luo on his pilgrimage to the Little Seamstress's village.

By the time we reached the perilous path Luo had told me about, the soft morning breeze had made way for a mountain gale. I gasped when I saw the risk Luo had been taking every day. Even I started trembling when I set foot on the ridge.

My left boot dislodged a stone, and almost at the same moment my right boot pushed some clods of earth over the side. They tumbled into the depths, and it was some time before we heard them hitting the bottom at different intervals. The sound reverberated into the distance, first on the right, then on the left.

I should never have looked down: to my right gaped a rocky crevasse of dizzying depth, at the bottom of which the trees were swathed in mist. My ears started buzzing when I looked to my left, where the earth had fallen away to create a sheer drop fifty metres deep.

Fortunately it was not quite as far over the ridge as Luo had said. On a boulder at the other end perched a raven with a red beak, its head ominously drawn into its shoulders.

'D'you want me to take your hod?' I offered casually. Luo was hanging back at the beginning of the path.

'Yes please, you take it.'

When I hoisted it onto my back I was buffeted by a blast of wind. The buzzing noise in my ears grew louder, and as I tossed my head to get rid of it I felt the stirrings of vertigo. At that point it was bearable, even slightly pleasant. I took a few steps. When I glanced over my shoulder I saw Luo still in the same place, his silhouette swaying gently like a tree in the wind.

Keeping my eyes resolutely fixed to the ground, I advanced with slow faltering steps like a tightrope walker. But when I was midway I saw the rocks ahead of me lurching to the right, then to the left, as if in an earthquake. Instinctively I bent down, and the vertigo did not subside until I was crouched low enough to steady myself with both hands. Rivulets of sweat trickled down my back, chest and forehead. I wiped my brow with the back of my hand, and was surprised at how cold the sweat was.

I looked over my shoulder again at Luo; he seemed to be calling out to me, but his voice was swallowed up by the buzzing in my head. Raising my eyes to avoid looking at the drop on either side of me, I saw the dark silhouette of a raven circling overhead, slowly flapping its wings in the dazzling sunlight.

'What can this mean?' I asked myself.

I couldn't move, and there, stuck in the middle of the ridge, I wondered what my good friend Jean-Christophe would say if I were to turn back. With an imperious wave of his conductor's baton he would tell me which way to go. He was unlikely to object to my beating a retreat in the face of death, I thought. After all, how could I die now, without having known love or sex, without having taken free individual action against the whole world, as he had?

I was filled with the desire to live. I turned full circle, still on my knees, and crawled back to the start. To lose my balance would have meant hurtling into the void and I clung to the earth for dear life. Suddenly I thought of Luo. He must have undergone the same ordeal, and yet he had succeeded in crossing to the other side.

His voice became clearer as the distance between us lessened. I noted that his face was deathly pale, as if he was even more frightened than I was. He called out to me, saying that I should straddle the ridge and drag myself forward that way. I took his advice, and this new position, though more humiliating, enabled me to reach him safely.

When I was back where I started I scrambled to my feet and set down the hod.

'Did you get stuck like this every day?' I asked him.

'No, just the first time.'

'Is it always there?'

'What?'

'The raven.'

I pointed my finger towards the red-beaked raven, which had now alighted on the ridge at the very spot where I had decided to turn around and go back.

'Yes, every morning, as if it has an appointment with me,' said Luo. 'But I never see it when I come back in the evening.'

I had no intention of making a fool of myself all over again, so I let Luo go on alone. He swung the hod onto his back and bent down slowly until his fingers were touching the ground. He then planted his hands firmly on the ridge one ahead of the other, and advanced steadily, his feet almost touching his hands with each step. After a while he paused and wiggled his bottom at me like a monkey balancing on the branch of a tree. The red-beaked raven took off and spiralled upwards, slowly beating its great wings.

Full of admiration, I watched Luo until he made it to the end of the ridge, which I was beginning to think of as purgatory, and disappeared behind some boulders. Suddenly I felt apprehensive about how his adventure with Balzac and the Little Seamstress would turn out. The big black bird had vanished, leaving an eerie silence on the mountain.

The next night I woke with a start.

It took me a while to work out where I was. In the

blackness I could hear the sound of regular breathing: Luo was asleep in the opposite bed. I groped around for a cigarette, and lit up. I was soothed by the unmistakable presence of the sow under the house on stilts, thrusting her snout against the walls of the pigsty, and then, like a speeded-up film, the dream I had just had came back to me in all its horror.

Luo was with a girl, and I was watching from afar as they teetered along a path with a chasm on either side. At first the girl, who was leading the way, was the daughter of the janitor at the hospital where our parents worked. A girl of our class, modest, ordinary, the kind of girl I had forgotten existed. Just as I was wondering what she could be doing there with Luo on the mountain, she turned into the Little Seamstress, vivacious, full of fun, shapely in a tight white T-shirt and black trousers. She wasn't walking across the ridge, she was prancing, while her young lover Luo followed behind on all fours. Neither of them was carrying a hod. The Little Seamstress's hair wasn't tied back into her usual long, thick pigtail, and as she ran her hair floated out over her shoulders like wings. I scanned the mountainside for the red-beaked raven, and when my eyes returned to my friends, the Little Seamstress had vanished. There was only Luo now, on his knees in the middle of the ridge, staring down the precipice on his right. He seemed to be calling out, but I couldn't hear a sound. Inexplicably, I found the courage to run over the ridge towards him. As I drew near it dawned on me that the Little Seamstress had fallen over the side. In spite of the almost sheer drop we slithered down the steep slope to the bottom, where we found her body on a bed of rock. She had folded double on impact, and her head had cracked wide open. There were two great gashes in the back of her skull, around which the blood was congealing. One of the gashes extended all the way to her finely turned forehead. Her mouth was twisted, the lips retracted to expose pink gums and clenched teeth, as if she was screaming, but there was no sound, only the smell of blood. When Luo took her in his arms I saw that he too was bleeding. Blood poured from his mouth, his left nostril, and one of his ears; it trickled down his arms and dripped onto the ground.

I told Luo about the nightmare, but he was unimpressed.

'Forget it,' he said. 'I've had quite a few of those dreams myself.'

He gathered up his jacket and the bamboo hod. I asked him: 'Will you warn the Little Seamstress to stay away from the ridge?'

'Of course not. She wants to come here, too, from time to time.'

'Tell her to wait a bit – at least until that wretched path has been cleared.'

'All right, I'll tell her.'

He was in a hurry and I almost felt jealous of his assignation with the doom-laden red-beaked raven.

'Don't tell her my dream, will you?'

'No fear.'

THE VILLAGE headman's return put a temporary halt to Luo's daily pilgrimages.

Neither the privilege of attending the Party conference nor his month of high life in town seemed to have given our headman much satisfaction. He had an aggrieved look, and his cheeks were swollen. His face contorted with rage as he fulminated against one of the revolutionary doctors at the district hospital: 'Son of a bitch, idiot barefoot doctor, pulled out a good tooth and left the bad one, which was next to it.' He was particularly furious that the haemorrhage following the extraction of the unoffending molar had prevented him from expressing his outrage, reduced as he was to garbling in a barely intelligible manner. He displayed the evidence of the operation to anyone who expressed the slightest sympathy for his misfortune: a blackened stump with a long pointed, yellow root, which he kept carefully wrapped in a square of red silk he had bought at a fair in Yong Jing.

The least sign of slackness was enough to incense him at this time, so for a while Luo and I set off dutifully each morning to work in the fields. We didn't even risk changing the time on our little magic alarm clock.

One evening the headman, still suffering from tooth-ache, turned up at our house while we were cooking supper. He unfolded the square of red silk in which he kept his tooth and held up a small lump of metal.

'This is pure tin, which I bought from a travelling salesman,' he told us. 'Hold it over a flame and it'll melt in fifteen minutes.'

Neither of us said anything. We were too busy suppressing our laughter at his exaggeratedly swollen cheeks. He could have walked straight out of a bad comic film.

'My dear Luo,' the headman said in an unfamiliar, wheedling tone, 'I'm sure you must have seen your father do it thousands of times: once the tin is malleable all you need to do is stuff a small quantity into the rotten tooth so that it kills the worms, isn't that right? You should know about these things, being the son of a well-known dentist. I'm counting on you to fix my tooth.'

'Are you serious? Do you want me to stopper your tooth with tin?'

'Yes I am. And if the pain goes away I'll give you a month off from work.'

This was a tempting prospect, but Luo felt obliged to dissuade him.

'Tin alone won't work,' he said. 'Besides, my father used modern equipment. He'd take a little electric drill and bore into the tooth to start with, before putting any filler in.'

The headman thought this over. He got up and left, muttering to himself: 'He's right. I saw them doing that at the district hospital. The cretin who pulled my good tooth also had a sort of thick needle whirring round and buzzing like a motor.'

A few days later, our headman's suffering was eclipsed by the arrival of the Little Seamstress's father. The morning sunlight glinted off his shiny sewing machine, which was carried aloft on the naked shoulders of a porter.

His annual visit to our village had been postponed several times, and it was unclear whether the delay was due to a surfeit of work or to a haphazard attitude to his schedule. At all events the villagers, to whom his arrival signalled happy times, were delighted to see the sinewy little man show up with his sparkling sewing machine, just a few weeks before the New Year.

As was his custom when he made his tour of the villages, he had left his daughter at home. When we had first set eyes on him on the narrow, slippery footpath, he had been in a sedan chair because of the rain and the mud. This time, however, the weather was sunny and he was travelling on foot, with a youthful energy that belied his years. He wore a faded green cap – no doubt the very same cap his daughter had lent me for our visit to the old miller – a loose-fitting blue jacket over a beige linen shirt with traditional frog fastening, and a glossy black belt made of genuine leather.

The whole village ran out to welcome him. The whoops of the children, the happy cries of the women shaking out lengths of material that had been stashed away for months, the occasional explosion of a leftover fire-cracker, and the excited grunts of the village swine all combined to create a festive atmosphere. He was mobbed by families pressing invitations on him, all hoping to be the first customer in line. But to everyone's profound astonishment, the old tailor declared: 'I will lodge with my daughter's young friends.'

We wondered what the hidden reason for this choice could be. The most likely explanation, we thought, was that he wanted to find out more about the young man who was his potential son-in-law. But, whatever his motives, his transformation of our house on stilts into a tailor's workshop meant that we bore witness to scenes of feminine intimacy such as we had never seen before. It was an on-going festival of almost anarchic proportions, with girls and women of all ages, plain ones and pretty ones, well off and poor, vying with each other over the fabrics, the lace trimmings, ribbons, buttons, even the sewing thread of their dream wardrobes. Watching them during fittings, Luo and I were amazed to see how agitated they were, how impatient, how physical their desire for new clothes was. It would evidently take more than a political regime, more than dire poverty to stop a woman from wanting to be well dressed: it was a desire as old as the world, as old as the desire for children.

Towards evening all the eggs, meat, vegetables and fruit that the villagers had presented to the old tailor like so many offerings were piled up in a corner of the room and the men came to join the crowd of women. The more timid ones sat by the fire, their bare heads bowed, cutting their hard toenails with curved knives. They hardly dared look at the girls. Other men, more experienced and more boisterous, joked with the women and made them obscene propositions. The old tailor's authority was sorely tried until, having grown weary and irritable, he ordered them out of the house.

The three of us had a quiet meal together, in the course of which we laughed at the memory of our first encounter on the mountain path. After our amicable supper I proposed entertaining our guest with some violin music before we all went to bed. His eyelids were drooping, and he declined the offer.

'Why don't you tell me a story instead,' he said, opening his mouth wide in a protracted yawn. 'The pair of you are excellent storytellers, so my daughter says. Which is why I insisted on staying in your house.'

It could have been because the mountain tailor was clearly tired, or because Luo didn't want his prospective father-in-law to think him too forward, but he seemed to think it was better if I did the honours.

'Go on,' he said encouragingly. 'Tell us something that I haven't heard before.'

It was with some reluctance that I agreed to take on the role of bedtime storyteller and, before embarking on my tale, I took the precaution of inviting my listeners to wash their feet with warm water and to slip under the covers in case they fell asleep before I finished. We got out two clean quilts, and tucked our guest into Luo's bed. The two of us then squeezed into mine together. It was time to begin. I extinguished the oil lamp to save on fuel, and, listening to the tailor's yawns grow louder and lengthier, I lay back with my head on my pillow, closed my eyes and waited for the opening words to come out of my mouth.

I would most certainly have opted for the story of a Chinese or North Korean film, or even an Albanian one, had I not tasted the forbidden fruit of Four-Eyes's secret suitcase. As it was, the stark proletarian realism of those stories, which had represented the sum total of my cultural education until a short while ago, struck me as being so far removed from human desires and true emotions, in short from real life, that there seemed little point in bothering

114

with them at this late hour. Suddenly the novel I had just finished reading flashed across my mind. I was confident that Luo had not yet read it: he was still completely wrapped up in Balzac.

I slid out from under the covers and sat at the foot of the bed, pondering the most difficult, delicate task: how to phrase my opening line. I wanted to set the tone with something straightforward and arresting.

'It is 1815, and we are in Marseilles.'

My voice rang out in the inky blackness of the room.

'Where's Marseilles?' the tailor interrupted sleepily.

'On the other side of the world. It's a major port in France.'

'Why do you want to take us so far away?'

'I was going to tell you a story about a French sailor. If the idea doesn't appeal to you, perhaps it would be better if we all had a rest now. Have a good night!'

In the dark Luo bent over and whispered softly: 'Well done!'

One or two minutes later I heard the tailor once more: 'What was your French sailor's name again?'

'He started out as Edmond Dantès, but later on he became the Count of Monte Cristo.'

'Cristo?'

'It's another name for Jesus, and it means the messiah, or saviour.'

And so I began to tell the story of Alexandre Dumas' novel. Luo interrupted me from time to time in a low voice, offering brief, intelligent comments. His enjoyment encouraged me, and soon the self-consciousness induced by the presence of our guest fell away. As for the tailor, he was not only weary after a hard day's work but also overwhelmed, no doubt, by all the foreign names and faraway places I mentioned. He didn't say another word; for all I knew he was fast asleep.

The artistry of the great Dumas was so compelling that I forgot all about our guest, and the words poured from me. My sentences became more precise, more concrete, more compact as I went along. I succeeded, with some effort, in sustaining the spare tone of the opening sentence. It was not an easy undertaking, but I was pleasantly surprised, in the course of telling the story, to see the narrative mechanism laid bare before my eyes: how Dumas established the theme of vengeance, and set out the different story-lines which he would eventually gather together with a firm, deft and audacious hand. It was like seeing a great, uprooted tree: the nobility of its trunk, the grandeur of its branches, the strength of its naked roots.

I lost all sense of time. How long had I been talking? An hour? Two? We had arrived at the point in the story where our hero, the French sailor, was locked up in a cell for the next twenty years. I felt drowsy, and had to stop.

'Right now,' Luo whispered to me, 'you're doing better than me. You should have been a writer.'

Intoxicated by this compliment, coming as it did from a master storyteller, I drifted off into a delicious sleep. Suddenly I heard the old tailor's voice rumbling in the dark.

'Why did you stop?'

'Pardon me!' I exclaimed. 'I thought you were asleep.'

'By no means. I've been listening all the time. I like your story.'

'I'm too tired to go on.'

'Well, try to keep it up just a little longer,' the old tailor pleaded.

'All right, just a little while,' I said. 'Do you remember where I left off?'

'He's been cast into the dungeon of a fortress on an island in the sea.'

I was impressed by the attentiveness of my elderly listener, and resumed my tale. Every half-hour or so I would pause, usually at a cliff-hanger, not because I was tired but because I couldn't resist showing off some tricks of the storyteller's trade. I made him beg me to go on. It was close to daybreak when we reached the part where the Abbot reveals the secret of the fabulous treasure hidden on the island of Monte Cristo and helps Edmond to escape from his miserable cell. The grey morning light seeped into the room through the chinks in the walls, to the accompanying twitter and warble of swallows, turtledoves and finches.

At the end of this sleepless night we all felt exhausted. The tailor had to donate a small sum of money to the village, to persuade the headman to give us time off from work.

'Have a good rest,' the old man said, winking at me, 'and make sure you are ready for my next rendezvous with the French sailor.'

It was the longest story I had ever told, for it took me nine whole nights to reach the end. It was a mystery to me where the old tailor found the energy to work during the day. Inevitably, some of the details he picked up from the French story started to have a discreet influence on the clothes he was making for the villagers. Dumas would have been most surprised to see the mountain men sporting sailor tops with square collars that flapped in the breeze. You could almost smell the briny Mediterranean air. The blue sailor trousers mentioned by Dumas and copied by his disciple the old tailor conquered the girls' hearts with their fluttering bell-bottoms and whiff of the Côte d'Azur. The tailor asked us to draw a five-pointed anchor, and for several years it became the most popular decorative feature in female fashion on Phoenix mountain. Some women went so far as to embroider tiny anchors on buttons with gold thread. But there were certain details in Dumas' novel that we kept to ourselves, such as the precise design of the embroidered lilies decorating the corsets and dresses worn by Mercedes. That was a secret we divulged exclusively to the tailor's daughter.

The third night of storytelling nearly ended in disaster. It was around five in the morning. We were at the very heart of the intrigue – the best part of all, in my view. The Count of Monte Cristo was back in Paris, and thanks to his shrewd manipulations he had succeeded in approaching his three sworn enemies, upon whom he sought revenge. One by one he moved his pawns in a game of diabolical ingenuity. Soon, the Prosecutor would be caught in the Count's carefully prepared snare. All of a sudden, just as the Count was about to fall in love with the Prosecutor's daughter, a dark shadowy figure loomed on the threshold holding a torch. The beam of light put the French Count to flight and brought us rapidly back to reality.

It was our village headman, wearing a cap. His swollen face was thrown into grotesque relief by the inky shadows cast on his face in the torchlight. We hadn't even heard his footsteps, so immersed we were in Dumas.

'Ah, what good wind has brought you here?' the tailor called out. 'I was wondering whether I would have the good fortune to meet you this year. I hear you have been suffering at the hands of an incompetent doctor.'

The headman did not deign to look at our guest – it was as if he hadn't noticed his presence. He trained his torch on my face.

'Anything wrong?' I asked.

'Come with me. We're going to have a talk in the Public Security Office at the commune headquarters.'

Although his toothache prevented him from shouting at me, his mumbling struck fear into my heart, for the name of the Security Office alone was enough to bring visions of torture and hell for any class enemy.

'What for?' I asked, lighting the oil lamp with trembling hands.

'You've been spreading reactionary trash. Just as well for our village that I never sleep, that I'm always on guard. I have been here since midnight listening to everything you've been saying, the whole reactionary story of Count Whatsisname.'

'It's all right,' Luo interjected, 'this Count isn't Chinese, you know.'

'I don't care. One day our revolution will triumph the world over! And anyone who bears the title of Count, regardless of his nationality, is by definition reactionary.'

'Wait, comrade,' Luo said. 'You don't know how the story began. Before passing himself off as an aristocrat, the man was a poor sailor, and seamen fall into the category of revolutionary workers – it says so in the "Little Red Book".'

'Don't waste my time with your stupid nonsense,' the headman retorted. 'Have you ever heard of a good man trying to get the better of a public prosecutor?'

Saying this, he spat on the floor, a sure sign that he would get violent if I didn't go with him.

I crawled out of bed, resigned to my fate, and put on

my sturdiest jacket and trousers, like someone preparing for a lengthy sojourn in prison. Emptying the pocket of my shirt I found some coins, which I handed to Luo so that they wouldn't fall into the hands of the Security Service thugs. Luo threw them on the bed.

'I'm coming with you,' he said.

'No, you stay here and take care of things as best you can.'

I had to fight back my tears as I spoke. The look in Luo's eyes told me that he had understood what I was trying to tell him: to keep the books well hidden in case I broke down under torture. I wasn't sure I would withstand the beatings and floggings that were said to be standard procedure during interrogations at the Security Office. My legs were quaking as I walked towards the headman. I felt as shaky as when I got into my first fight as a boy: I had lunged at my adversary in a show of bravery, but the shameful trembling of my legs had given me away.

The headman's breath smelt of decay. His small eyes, one of them marked as always by three blood spots, fixed me in a savage stare. For a moment I thought he was going to grab me by the collar and hurl me down the ladder. But he just stood there, rooted to the spot. Finally his eyes left me, rested briefly on the bars of the bed, and then bored into Luo, whom he asked: 'You remember the piece of tin I showed you?'

'Not very well,' Luo replied, puzzled.

'The little thing I asked you to stuff into my bad tooth.'

'Yes, I remember now.'

'I still have it,' the headman said, taking the red silk parcel out of his coat pocket.

'I don't get your meaning,' Luo said, still mystified.

'If you, the son of a great dentist, can cure my tooth, I'll leave your friend here alone. If not, I'll march him straight to the Security Office and report him for spreading reactionary filth.'

THE HEADMAN'S teeth resembled a jagged mountain range. Three incisors protruded from blackened inflamed gums like flakes of prehistoric basalt, while his tobacco-stained canines were like snaggled rocks of diluvian travertine. As for the molars, some of them had such deep grooves on the crown that – the dentist's son declared with an appropriately scientific air – the owner must have suffered a bout of syphilis. The headman averted his face, without contradicting the diagnosis.

The troublesome tooth was all the way at the back of his jaw, next to the dark pulpy hole left by its extracted neighbour. It was a solitary, decayed wisdom tooth, as porous as a coral reef. The headman kept caressing it with his yellow tongue which would then explore the hole next to it and finish with a consoling click against the roof of his mouth.

The perambulations of this slimy tongue were interrupted by a thick steel sewing machine needle which entered the headman's mouth and hovered above the affected tooth. The tongue was immediately attracted to the intruder, and ran its tip up and down the cold, foreign object. It trembled, drew back, then reared up for a fresh sally, and, excited by the unfamiliar sensation, licked the needle again with almost voluptuous abandon.

The old tailor pressed his foot on the treadle of the sewing machine, and the up-and-down motion set the needle, which was attached by a string to the driving wheel, spinning round. The headman's tongue recoiled in alarm. Luo, steadying the makeshift drill between the tips of his fingers, adjusted the position of his hand. He waited a few seconds for the treadle to speed up, then attacked the tooth with the needle, eliciting an ear-splitting shriek from the patient. No sooner had Luo withdrawn the needle than the headman rolled off the bed that we had set up next to the sewing machine.

'You nearly killed me!' he fumed. 'What d'you think you're doing?'

'I warned you,' the tailor said. 'I've seen them do this kind of thing at country fairs. Anyway, it was you who insisted on making us do this.'

'Well, it hurts like hell,' said the headman.

'It's bound to be painful,' Luo said. 'Do you realise the speed of an electric drill in a proper hospital? It's hundreds of rotations per second. The slower it turns, the more painful it is.'

'Try again,' the headman said resolutely, adjusting his cap. 'I've gone without sleep and food for a whole week already. Better to deal with this once and for all.'

He shut his eyes to avoid seeing the needle enter his mouth, but the result was the same as before. The excruciating pain propelled him off the bed with the needle still stuck in his tooth.

His violent reaction almost upset the oil lamp, over which I was softening the lump of tin on a spoon.

It was an absurd situation, but no one dared to laugh, for fear of raising the subject of my arrest.

Luo retrieved the needle, wiped it, inspected it closely, then suggested the patient rinse his mouth with a glass of water. The headman complied, and spat out the liquid onto the floor next to his cap, which had slipped off his head. The water was pink.

The old tailor seemed astonished. 'You're bleeding,' he said.

'If you want me to fix your tooth,' Luo said, reaching for the fallen cap and replacing it on the headman's rumpled hair, 'I can't see any other way than to tie you to the bed.'

'Strap me down?' the headman cried indignantly. 'You forget that I've got the commune leader's mandate.'

'But as your body is refusing to collaborate, I'm afraid we'll have to take extreme measures.'

I was flabbergasted. How could this tyrant, this political and economic despot, this police chief, ever resign himself to being restrained in this way, which was not only humiliating but also made him look utterly ridiculous? What the devil had got into him? I had no time to ponder the question then, and even today it confounds me. As it was, Luo quickly strapped him down on the bed, and the tailor, charged with the awesome task of gripping the patient's head with both hands to keep it still, indicated that I should take his place working the treadle.

This new responsibility filled me with trepidation. I took my shoes off, placed the ball of my foot on the treadle and braced myself.

At a sign from Luo I set the drive wheel in motion, and soon my feet were pedalling away to the relentless rhythm of the machine. I accelerated, feeling like a cyclist racing at full tilt; the needle juddered, trembled, made contact once more with the treacherous tooth, whereupon a dreadful gurgling noise rose from the throat of the immobilised headman. Not only was he lashed to the bed with a length of strong rope, like a bad guy in a film about to get his comeuppance, but his head was clamped in the old tailor's vice-like grip. His face was deathly pale and he was foaming at the mouth.

Suddenly, I felt the stirrings of an uncontrollably sadistic impulse, like a volcano about to erupt. I thought about all the miseries of re-education, and slowed down the pace of the treadle.

Luo shot me a glance of complicity.

I pedalled even more slowly, this time to punish him for threatening to take me into custody. It was as if the drill were about to break down. It was barely moving now, making just one rotation per second, maybe two – who knows? Eventually, having penetrated the decay, the steel point made a final tremor and came to a complete standstill as I lifted my feet off the treadle altogether like a cyclist freewheeling downhill. For a moment the suspense was agonising. I put on an air of innocent, calm deliberation to disguise the hatred smouldering in my eyes, and bent down in a pretence of checking whether the belt was still properly laid over the drive wheel. Then I replaced my feet on the treadle and the needle began to turn again, slowly and shakily, as if the cyclist were struggling up a steep slope. It became a chisel, cutting into a ghastly prehistoric rock face and releasing little puffs of greasy yellow dust. I had turned into a sadist – an out-and-out sadist.

THE OLD MILLER'S STORY

Yes indeed, I saw the two of them, both as naked as worms. I had gone to cut firewood down in the valley, as is my custom. I go there once a week, and always pass the waterfall. Where is it exactly? A kilometre or two away from my mill, or thereabouts. The torrent cascades onto some boulders twenty metres below and forms a deep pool of green water. It is quite far from the pathway, so people seldom find it.

I didn't see them at once, but the birds roosting on the rocky promontories seemed to have been startled by something; they flew up and passed noisily over my head.

Yes, they were ravens with red beaks – how did you guess? There must have been a dozen in all. One of them – perhaps it was more aggressive than the others, or more incensed at the disturbance – swooped down towards me, brushing my face with the tip of its wing. I can still remember the stench of it.

Because of the birds I took a detour and went down to the pool to see what had frightened them. It was there that

I saw them, their heads above the surface. They must have plunged into the water from a high rock and made a loud splash, sending the ravens into flight.

Your interpreter? No, I did not recognise him at once. I followed the two figures with my eyes, their bodies entwined, whirling round and round in the water. It was such an amazing sight that it took me a long while to realise that they were not simply swimming together. No indeed! They were coupling under water.

What did you say? Copulating? That word is too learned for the likes of me. Here on the mountain we talk about coupling. I had no intention of spying on them. My old face reddened. I had never seen such a thing in my life – people making love while swimming. I was rooted to the spot. You know that at my age one is defenceless. They swam out of the deep water into the shallows and lay on a bed of stones where the limpid water glittering in the sun exaggerated and distorted their obscene movements.

I felt ashamed, it is true, not because I could not take my eyes off them, but because I was so keenly aware of being an old man whose body was limp where it was not bony. I understood full well that I would never taste the watery delights enjoyed by them.

Afterwards, the girl gathered some leaves and fashioned a loincloth, which she tied round her hips. She did not seem as tired as her friend – quite the contrary. She was brimming with energy, and clambered along the surrounding rocks. From time to time she vanished behind a boulder covered in green moss and then reappeared on top of another, as if she had emerged from a fissure in the rock. She adjusted her loincloth so as to conceal her private parts, and set about climbing up to a ledge about ten metres above the pool.

Of course, she could not see me. I had been very discreet, keeping myself hidden behind a leafy bush. I didn't know who the girl was; she had evidently never visited my mill. When she was standing on the rocky ledge overhead, I was close enough to admire her naked, dripping body. She stood there fiddling with her loincloth, sliding it over her naked belly and under her firm, rosy-tipped breasts.

The red-beaked ravens returned, alighting all around her on the high, narrow ledge.

All of a sudden she brushed them aside with her feet and took a few steps back. Then she rushed forward for a great leap into space, her arms outstretched like the wings of a swallow sailing on the breeze.

The ravens followed suit. But before soaring into the sky they dived down alongside the girl's flying body. She had become a swallow. Her wings, extended, did not fold until she touched the surface of the water and plummeted into the depths.

I looked around for her friend, and saw him sitting naked on the shore, eyes closed, lolling against a rock. The secret part of his body was shrunken and sleeping.

The thought flashed across my mind that I had seen the young man before, but I could not remember when. It was not until I was in the forest chopping down a tree that it hit me: the young man was the interpreter who accompanied you when you visited me a few months ago.

It was lucky for him, your make-believe interpreter, that it was I who saw him, for I am not easily shocked, and have never denounced anyone to the Public Security Office. If it had been anyone else he would have been in deep trouble, believe me.

LUO'S STORY

What can I say? That she's a good swimmer? Sure, she swims like a dolphin now. She used to swim the way peasants do, using only her arms, not her legs. Before I showed her how to do the breaststroke she could only do doggy paddle. But she has the physique of a true swimmer. There were only two or three things I had to teach her. She's even mastered the butterfly stroke: arms flung out, lower body undulating, torso rising up out of the water in a perfect aerodynamic curve, and legs churning the water like the tail of a dolphin.

What she has discovered all on her own is how to dive from dangerous heights. I have never dared do it – I have a horror of heights. When we're in our watery paradise – a deep secluded pool – and she climbs up to a high ledge to jump off, I always stay down below. Looking up to see her spring for an almost perpendicular dive makes me so dizzy that the ledge and the towering gingkos behind blur into one. Her tiny figure is like a fruit growing at the top of a tree. She calls out to me, but the sound is drowned out by the torrent cascading onto the rocks. Suddenly, the fruit falls, streaking through the air towards me, slicing the surface of the water like an arrow with barely a splash.

In the days before his detention, my father used to say that dancing was not something that could be taught, and he was right. The same is true of diving and writing poetry, for the best divers and poets are self-taught. Some people can spend their lives having lessons and still resemble stones when they hurtle through the air. They never achieve the lightness of dropping fruit.

I had a key ring, a birthday present from my mother when I was a boy. It was gold-plated, and decorated with tiny jade leaves. I always carried it with me, it was my talisman to ward off misfortune. It held a whole bunch of keys, although I had no possessions that needed locking up. There were the keys to our house in Chengdu, to the drawer with my personal belongings in my mother's cabinet, to the back door at home, as well as a penknife and a nail clipper. Not long ago I added the master-key that we used to get into Four-Eyes's house to steal the books. I treasured it as a souvenir of a successful break-in.

One afternoon in September, the two of us clambered down to our pool. As usual, the place was deserted. The water felt a little cold, so I read her a chapter of *Lost Illusions*. I was less taken with this book of Balzac's than with *Père Goriot*, and yet, when she caught a tortoise among the rocks in the shallows, it was this novel that inspired me to take my penknife and carve the long-nosed profiles of the two ambitious main characters on the creature's shell, before releasing it.

The tortoise scuttled away. Suddenly I wondered: 'Who will ever release me from this mountain?'

This question, although pointless, plunged me into the

depths of despair. As I folded up my penknife and added it to the keys jangling on the ring, those Chengdu keys that I probably wouldn't use ever again, I had a lump in my throat. I envied the tortoise its freedom. With a heavy heart I flung my key ring into the pool.

Her reaction was instantaneous. She surged forward with a masterful butterfly stroke and dived down in pursuit of my key ring. She was submerged for such a long time that I got very agitated. The dark surface of the pool was strangely still, almost sinister; there was not a bubble to be seen. I shouted 'Where are you for God's sake?' I called out her name, and also her nickname, 'Little Seamstress', then I plunged down to the bottom of the pool. There she was, before my very eyes, rising upwards with dolphin-like undulations. I was stunned by the grace of her sinuous body and her long hair rippling in the water. It was a beautiful sight.

When we reached the surface I saw my key ring between her lips, glistening with beads of water.

She must have been the only person in the world who still had faith in my ultimate release from re-education, who was convinced that I would need my keys again some day.

From then on we played the key ring game each time we went to the secluded mountain pool. I loved it, not because I had any illusions about my future, but simply because it gave me the opportunity to admire her sensual body gliding through the water naked but for the fragile leaves of her loincloth.

Today, however, we lost the key ring in the depths of the pool. I should have stopped her from going down again to look for it when I knew it was dangerous. Luckily it didn't turn out too disastrously, but I never want to set foot in that place again.

When I got back to the village this evening I found a telegram waiting for me, saying that my mother has been rushed to hospital and that I must come as soon as possible.

The village headman, no doubt mellowed by the success of his dental treatment, has given me permission to spend a month at my mother's sickbed. I am to leave in the morning. How ironic that I shall be returning to my parents' house without my keys.

THE LITTLE SEAMSTRESS'S STORY

The books Luo read to me always made me want to dive into the cool water of the mountain torrent. Why? It was a gut reaction. Like when you can't help blurting out what you're thinking.

At the bottom of the pool there was a bluish blur, a swathe of murkiness where you couldn't make out the details of the underwater scenery. As if there was a veil before your eyes. Luckily Luo's key ring always landed in more or less the same place in the middle, within a circle a few metres wide. There were stones on the bottom, which you didn't even notice until you touched them; some of them were small and smooth, like pale eggs, and they had lain there for years and years, centuries even, probably. Others were as big as human heads, among which there were some with strangely jutting curves like buffalo horns. From time to time, although not very often, you'd come across stones that were sharp and jagged, which lay in wait for you with their barbed edges ready to pierce your skin and make you bleed. There were also shells, deeply embedded in the clayey bottom. Goodness knows where they came from. They had clotted together to form rocks blanketed with tender moss, but you could still tell they were shells.

What's that you're saying? Why I enjoyed diving down to retrieve his key ring? I know what you're getting at – you think I'm like a silly dog that keeps running to fetch the stick thrown by its master. I'm not like those young French girls Balzac talks about. I'm a mountain girl. I just love pleasing Luo, that's all there is to it.

You want me to tell you what happened the last time we were there? It was a week ago, at least. It was just before Luo got that telegram about his mother being ill. We arrived at the pool towards noon. We had a dip, but didn't stay in the water very long, just long enough for a little fun. I had brought along some corn bread, eggs and fruit, and while we were having our picnic Luo told me some more about the French sailor who became a Count – the one my father is such an admirer of. Luo only recounted a little scene – you know, the one where the Count finally meets the woman he loved when he was young, and same girl on whose account he was sentenced to twenty years in prison. She pretends not to recognise him, and she does so with such conviction that you'd swear she had truly forgotten her past. Oh, it was heart-breaking!

We wanted to take a little siesta, but I was kept wide awake thinking about this tragic encounter. You know what we did? The two of us acted out the whole reunion scene, with Luo as Monte Cristo and me as his former fiancée. It was fantastic. There I was, improvising away, saying all sorts of things off the top of my head. As for Luo, he played his part to the hilt. The Count was still in love with me. My words mortally wounded him, poor thing, you could tell from the expression on his face. He glared at me, his eyes ablaze with hatred and rage as if I were the girl who had married the man who had betrayed him.

It was a totally new experience for me. Before, I had no idea that you could take on the role of a completely different person, actually become that person – a rich lady, for example – and still be your own self. Luo told me I'd make a good actress.

After our acting session it was time for our usual game. Luo flung his key ring into the water, and it sank like a pebble. I stepped into the pool and ducked under the surface. I ran my fingers over the stony bed and groped in shadowy recesses where the water was almost black until, suddenly, I touched a snake. It was ages since I had touched a snake, either on land or underwater, but its slippery cold skin was instantly recognisable. I shrank back instinctively and quickly headed to the shore.

Where did it come from? It is impossible to say. It may have been carried down by the stream, or it may have been a grass snake in search of new territory.

A few minutes later I plunged in again, in spite of Luo's protestations. I couldn't bear to think of his keys being left to a snake.

But this time I was worried. Knowing the snake was there was very frightening: even in the water I could feel the cold sweat running over my back. The motionless stones on the bottom suddenly seemed to come alive, turning into horrible creatures out to get me. I rose up to the surface again to take another deep breath.

The third time I very nearly succeeded. I spotted the key ring at last glimmering on the bottom of the pool, but when I reached out to grab it I felt a stinging blow to my right hand: a snapping of jaws, fierce and very painful. After that I gave up trying to retrieve Luo's key ring.

Fifty years from now the ugly scar will still be there, on my middle finger. Go on, feel it.

L UO WAS away on his month's leave.

I enjoyed being on my own occasionally to do whatever I pleased, to eat what I wanted when I felt like it. Indeed I would have had a wonderful time being the sole lord and master of our house on stilts, if Luo hadn't entrusted me with a delicate mission on the eve of his departure.

'I want you to do me a favour,' he had said conspiratorially. 'While I'm away, would you guard the Little Seamstress for me?'

He said she had a lot of admirers on the mountain, including a fair number of city youths, and that during his month's absence they would make a beeline for the tailor's workshop in a bid to win her favour. 'You mustn't forget,' he admonished, 'that she's the Number One beauty on the Phoenix of the Sky.' My task was to spend as much time as I could at her side, to serve as the guardian of her affections so to speak. I was to prevent any contenders from insinuating themselves into her private life, from sneaking into a domain to which only Luo, my beloved commander, was rightfully entitled.

I was surprised and flattered by his request, and promised to do as he instructed. How blindly Luo trusted me! Asking this of me at the last minute was like giving me a priceless treasure for safekeeping, without it even entering his head that I might make off with it myself.

At the time my sole preoccupation was to honour the faith he had in me. I pictured myself at the head of a routed army, charged with escorting the young wife of my bosom friend, the commander-in-chief, across a vast, bleak desert. Armed with pistol and machine gun I'd stand guard every night over the tent in which the gracious lady slept, and I'd ward off the horrible savages lusting after her flesh while their eyes, burning with desire, flashed in the dark. After one month of the most excruciating hardship – sandstorms, shortages of food and water, soldiers beginning to mutiny – we'd reach the end of the desert, and just as the young lady ran to her beloved, just as she and my friend fell into each other's arms at last, I'd faint from exhaustion and thirst on the crest of the last sand dune.

And so, from the day Luo left the village to visit his mother in the city, I assumed the role of undercover agent. Each morning I headed down the mountainside to the village where the Little Seamstress lived. My look was steely and my pace brisk, as befitting a secret agent with a mission. Autumn had arrived, and the secret agent bowled along the mountain path like a vessel in full sail. The path skirted the village where Four-Eyes had been lodged and then made a northbound turn, and the secret agent had to struggle against heavy winds, hunched over, head bowed, like an indefatigable mountaineer. Upon reaching the perilous ridge with the yawning chasm on either side he would slow his pace a little, without, however, having to crouch down and crawl on his hands and knees. Day after day he conquered his vertigo. He wavered only slightly as he advanced, and fastened his gaze on the cold beady eyes of the red-beaked raven which was perched, as always, on top of the boulder at the other end of the crossing.

Misplacing just one step would mean losing his footing altogether, which would send the tightrope walker crashing to his death on the bottom of either the left chasm or the right.

Did our undercover agent address the raven, did he offer it a crust of bread? I don't suppose he did. He was certainly perturbed by the bird's cool, impassive gaze, and the image of it did not fade from his memory until many years later. Such aloofness, he felt, was a mark of the supernatural. But he was not deterred: his mind was made up and he would accomplish his mission.

It is important to note that the bamboo hod, formerly carried by Luo, now rested on the back of our secret agent. As usual it contained, safely stashed under leaves, vegetables, rice stalks or maize cobs, a novel by Balzac translated by Fu Lei. Some mornings, when the clouds hung low in the sky, you would have sworn it was a bamboo hod and not a man ascending the path and vanishing into the grey mist.

The Little Seamstress was not aware that she was under surveillance − to her I was merely a substitute reader.

I couldn't help noticing that she enjoyed listening to me. She even seemed to appreciate my way of reading the story more than my predecessor's. Reading aloud whole pages word for word struck me as pretty boring, so I decided to take a different approach. I would start by reading a couple of pages or a short chapter while she did her work on the sewing machine. Then, after allowing some time for it to sink in, I would ask her what she thought would happen next. Once she had answered my question I would tell her what it said in the book, almost paragraph by paragraph. I couldn't resist taking slight liberties, adding bits here and there by way of a personal touch to make the story more interesting to her. When I felt good old Balzac was running out of steam I would contribute little inventions of my own, or even insert whole scenes from another novel.

It is time to dwell for a moment on the life led by the founder of this tailoring dynasty, the master of the workshop. Between visits to clients in the surrounding villages the old tailor would spend some time at home, although quite often he would have to leave again after two or three days. He was soon accustomed to my daily attendance at his house. What's more, the swarm of suitors pretending to be customers were kept at bay by his presence, and he became a trusty accomplice to my secret mission. He hadn't forgotten the nine nights he had spent at our house on stilts, listening to *The Count of Monte Cristo*. The experience was repeated in his own home. Not quite so spellbound, perhaps, but still eager, he listened to some more Balzac: *Cousin Pons*, this time, a rather dark tale. By chance he was at home for three nights in a row at the point where Cibot the tailor, a minor character in the book, is kept in suspense by Remonencq the scrap-iron merchant.

Never had a secret agent carried out his mission with more dedication. Between chapters of *Cousin Pons* I would volunteer to do chores about the house. It was I for instance who would take two large wooden buckets to the communal well to replenish the household reservoir. And quite often I did the cooking, too. I took great pleasure in these humble tasks, cleaning vegetables and cutting meat with the fastidiousness of a true chef. I would chop wood with a blunt hatchet, arrange the logs with care to ensure that they would burn properly. And when the fire threatened to go out, which was often, I had no qualms about crouching down in clouds of suffocating smoke to blow on the embers with adolescent impatience. The days sped by. It was not long before I took it upon myself, out of a sense of courtesy and respect for womanhood that I had learned from Balzac, to relieve the Little Seamstress of her laundering duties, and whenever she was up to her eyes in work I would brave the cold of approaching winter and go down to the stream to wash clothes.

This voluntary domestication on my part not only softened my temperament but also gave me more intimate access to the female realm. Balsam, does that ring a bell? It's a common plant you find in florists' shops or growing in window boxes. The blooms are sometimes yellow but more often crimson, and ripen into fat berries which burst open at the slightest touch, releasing a spray of seeds. The balsam flower was the imperial emblem of Phoenix mountain, for in the shape of its showy petals and spur one can see the head, wings, feet and even the tail feathers of that mythical bird.

One late afternoon – the light was already fading – we found ourselves alone in the privacy of the kitchen. Sheltered from curious eyes, the secret agent assumed yet another identity. Already a storyteller, cook and laundry-man, the factotum now became a manicurist as well: after rinsing the Little Seamstress's fingers in a wooden basin he lovingly applied the thick juice of crushed balsam flowers to each of her nails in turn.

Her hands bore no resemblance to those of a peasant, for they were not gnarled by field work. There was a pink scar on the middle finger of her right hand – no doubt from the snakebite she had received in the mountain pool.

'Where did you learn all this girlish stuff?' the Little Seamstress asked.

'From my mother. According to her, if you leave the rags I've wrapped round your fingertips on overnight, you'll find your nails stained bright red, as if you'd varnished them.'

'How long will they stay red?'

'Ten days or so.'

I longed to ask if I might kiss her red nails when I returned the next day, as a reward for my artistic endeavour, but the pink scar on her finger brought me down to earth with a thud. I reminded myself of the prohibitions arising from my gallant commitment to my friend and commander.

That evening, when I left her house with *Cousin Pons* safely secreted in my bamboo hod, I was made keenly aware of the jealousy gnawing at the hearts of the local bachelors. Hardly had I set out along the path than I noticed a crowd of about fifteen yokels gathering behind my back and following me in silence.

Glancing over my shoulder, I was taken aback by the hostility on their young faces. I quickened my pace.

The silence was broken by a jeering voice behind my back, exaggerating the city accent: 'Please Little Seamstress, let me wash your clothes!'

I blushed and turned my head to see who was parodying me: it was the village cripple, the eldest in the group. He was brandishing a catapult.

I decided to ignore the affront, and proceeded on my way while the group came closer, jostling me and chanting the cripple's taunt amid roars of aggressive, sneering laughter.

Their mockery grew more savage until one of them stabbed his finger at me, shouting the ultimate insult: 'Dirty dog – so you like washing her panties, eh?'

I was shocked. How had they found out? I couldn't utter another word, nor hide my embarrassment, because I had in fact washed her underwear on one occasion.

The cripple stepped out in front of me, barring my way. He stripped off his trousers and then his underpants, exposing his bushy, flaccid private parts.

'Here, take them! You can wash mine too!' he jeered. An obscene grin spread over his face, which was contorted with excitement. He held up the grimy, stained underpants and waved them triumphantly over his head.

I racked my brains for something to say, but I was so enraged, so utterly stunned, that I couldn't come up with a suitably damning imprecation. I was shaking all over, and close to tears.

I have only a vague memory of what happened next. But I do know that I braced myself and swung my hod at the cripple. I wanted to strike him in the face, but he managed to dodge the blow, which landed on his right shoulder. In the ensuing scuffle I was very quickly brought to my knees, with two young thugs holding me down. My hod slipped from my grasp and rolled over the ground, spilling the contents: the two eggs I had wrapped in a cabbage leaf had broken and were leaking onto the cover of *Cousin Pons*. The book lay in the dust for all to see.

A hush descended. Although illiterate, my tormentors, or rather the Little Seamstress's swarm of disappointed suitors, were flabbergasted by the sight of this recondite object: a book. They all crowded round for a closer look – all except the two holding me fast, that is.

The bare-bottomed cripple sank onto his haunches and opened the book at the frontispiece. He stared at the black and white portrait of Balzac wearing a long beard and silvery moustache.

'Is that Karl Marx?' someone asked the cripple. 'You should know, you've travelled more than us.'

The cripple did not reply at once.

'Or is it Lenin?' another yokel asked.

'Or Stalin, without his uniform?'

Taking advantage of the general confusion, I wrenched myself free from my keepers' grasp and with a mighty shove I parted the crowd and lunged at my book, yelling: 'Don't touch!' as if it were an explosive device about to go off.

Before the cripple had time to realise what was happening I snatched the book from his hands and made a run for it.

A volley of stones and jibes followed in my wake. 'Filthy panty-washer! Coward! We'll give you some re-education all right, just you wait!' A missile from their catapult struck me on my left ear. I felt a stab of pain and suddenly lost my hearing on that side. I reached up to touch my ear, and my fingers came away dripping with blood.

Behind me the insults grew both louder and more obscene. The baying voices bounced off the rocky cliffs and resounded in the valleys, their tone becoming increasingly menacing, as if they were preparing for a fresh assault or even a lynching. Eventually the noise died down, and silence reigned once more.

On his way home that evening the injured secret agent

decided ruefully that his mission would be impossible to accomplish.

That night seemed never-ending. The house on stilts seemed lonelier, bleaker, more damp-ridden than ever. A smell of desolation hung in the air. It was an unmistakable smell: cold, rancid, moist. You would have sworn the place had been deserted for a long time. In an attempt to forget the pain in my left ear, I settled down to reread my favourite novel, *Jean-Christophe*. I had lit several oil lamps for consolation, but even their reeking flames did not dispel the oppressive smell, and my gloom deepened.

My ear had stopped bleeding, but it was bruised and swollen, and the pain was so severe that I found it impossible to concentrate on my book. When I raised my hand gingerly to touch the bruise I was flooded with rage all over again.

What a night! I remember it vividly, but even after all these years I still don't wholly understand my reaction. All through the night the pain in my ear kept me awake and thrashing about on my bed, which seemed strewn with needles. Instead of thinking up ways to avenge myself – for instance by chopping off the cripple's ears – I kept imagining that I was being attacked anew by the same gang of yokels. I pictured myself being tied to a tree while they crowded round, punching me and torturing me. The last rays of the setting sun glinted off the blade of a knife, which was being brandished by the cripple. It was unlike the traditional butcher's knife, for its blade was strangely long and pointed. The cripple ran his fingers along the blade, caressing it, then raised the knife and sliced off my left ear in one fell swoop, without a sound. My ear dropped to the ground and bounced, while my assailant wiped the blood off the long blade. I was saved from further torment by the arrival of the Little Seamstress, weeping profusely. The gang fled.

Then I imagined myself being untied by the mountain girl with her crimson, balsam-stained nails. She allowed me to take her fingers in my mouth and to lick them lovingly. How sweet the taste was! The thick balsam juice coating her glossy nails gave off a musky fragrance, which roused my carnal instincts. Moistened by my saliva, the crimson dye blazed even more brightly, and then, like an erupting volcano, it softened and liquefied into a flow of hissing, red-hot lava sliding over my tongue, overflowing my lips.

Once unleashed, the lava rolled down my chin, forming rivulets on my bruised shoulders, lingering on the flat stretch of my chest, circling my nipples, snaking down towards my waist, pausing at my navel before entering me and meandering through my veins and entrails, licking and probing its way to the seat of my manhood where the blood boiled, anarchic and self-willed, in total disregard of the tight restrictions which the secret agent had so mistakenly imposed upon himself.

The last oil lamp flickered and died for lack of fuel, leaving the secret agent lying face down on his bed, where he abandoned himself in the dark to a betrayal that left his pants sticky.

The luminous hands of the alarm clock indicated midnight.

'I'M IN trouble,' said the Little Seamstress.

It was the morning after my encounter with the randy suitors. We were in the kitchen at her house, wreathed in greeny-yellow steam and the aroma of rice cooking in the pan; she was chopping vegetables and I was tending the fire. We could hear the familiar, regular whirr of the sewing machine next door, where her father was at work. Neither he nor his daughter seemed to be aware of what had happened to me. To my surprise, they took no notice of the bruising on my left ear. I was so busy trying to think of some excuse for discontinuing my daily visits that I didn't pay attention to what she was saying.

'I've got a problem,' she repeated.

'What, with the cripple and his gang?'

'No.'

'With Luo?' I asked, feeling a sneaky ray of hope.

'It's not that either,' she said morosely. 'I feel guilty, but it's too late now.'

'What are you on about?'

'I've been throwing up. Even this morning. It must be morning sickness.'

My heart sank to see the tears well up in her eyes, trickle quietly down her cheeks and drip all over the leaves of the vegetables and onto her hands with their crimson-tipped fingers.

'My father will kill him when he finds out,' she moaned, struggling to keep her voice down.

She had missed two periods. She hadn't mentioned this to Luo, although it was he who was responsible – or to blame. When he left the mountain the previous month she was not yet worried.

I was more aghast at the unexpected show of emotion than at the news she had just confided in me, for it was not like her to break down and cry. Seeing her anguish was more than I could bear, and I would have thrown my arms around her to console her had not the whirr of the sewing machine next door quickly brought me back to my senses.

Besides, it was hard to see how she might be consoled. Although I knew virtually nothing about sex at the time, I did know what it meant to miss two periods in a row.

Her distress was infectious, and soon I too was shedding tears, although I hid them from her. I felt as if it were my child that she was carrying, as if it had been me and not Luo making love to her under the majestic gingko tree and in the limpid water of the secret pool. I was deeply moved; she was my soul mate and I was ready to spend the rest of my life taking care of her, content even to die a bachelor if that would help. Or I would have married her myself, had the law permitted it – even if it meant a chaste marriage – so that she could give birth legitimately to my friend's child.

I glanced at her stomach, but it was hidden under her red, hand-knitted woolly jumper, and all I could see was her body convulsing with stifled sobs. Once a woman starts crying over missed periods there's no stopping her, they say. A pang of fear shot through me, and I felt weak at the knees.

I forgot to ask the most pressing question, that is, whether she wanted to be a teenage mother. The reason for this omission on my part was simple: there was not the slightest chance of her being allowed to keep the child anyway. There was not a hospital, doctor or midwife to be found in these parts who could be persuaded to break the law by offering assistance to an unmarried woman in labour. And Luo wouldn't be able to marry the Little Seamstress for several years, given that marriage under the age of twenty-five was illegal. The situation was hopeless. There was nowhere for them to go, for there was no conceivable place where a Romeo and his pregnant Juliet might elude the long arm of the law, nor indeed where they might live the life of Robinson Crusoe attended by a secret agent turned Man Friday. Every nook and cranny of the land came under the all-seeing eye of the dictatorship of the proletariat, which had cast its gigantic, fine-meshed net over the whole of China.

When she had calmed down a little we went over all the ways of procuring an abortion that we could think of. We discussed the subject again and again behind her father's back, racking our brains for some solution that would be discreet enough to save the couple from disgrace in the eyes of the people as well as from political and administrative punishment. The law seemed to have been expressly designed to make things impossible for them: they couldn't go ahead and have the child before marrying, and the law prohibited abortion.

At this moment of emotional upheaval I could not help admiring my friend Luo's foresight in appointing me as her guardian. Since my mission included protecting her from bodily harm, I summoned every means of persuasion to stop her from running to the sorceresses for a herbal remedy, for she risked not only being poisoned but also denounced. I was also able to convince her that jumping off the roof of her house in the hope of provoking a miscarriage was a very bad idea, for she might end up a cripple, in which case she would be condemned to marry the other cripple in her village.

Eventually we decided that I should go on a reconnaissance trip to the town of Yong Jing, where I would sound out the hospital for ways of getting help from the gynaecology department.

Although Yong Jing was the district capital, it was so small, as you no doubt remember, that whenever the canteen served beef and onions you could smell it all over town. The modest hospital stood on a hillside, past the high school basketball court which did service as open-air cinema. It consisted of two buildings. The first, reserved for outpatients, was at the foot of the hill, and over the entrance it boasted an enormous portrait of a uniformed Chairman Mao waving his hand towards a multitude of waiting patients with whimpering children in tow. Further up on the hill stood a three-storey building in white-washed brick, without balconies. It was there that the inpatients were housed.

And so, after two days of tramping across the mountain and one sleepless night in a lice-ridden inn, I slipped into the clinic where the specialist staff had their consulting rooms. The better to blend in with the peasant folk, I was wearing my old sheepskin coat. However, as soon as I set foot in the medical atmosphere that had been so familiar to me since childhood, I became very apprehensive and broke out in a sweat. On the ground floor, at the end of a narrow, dimly lit corridor where the air was tainted with a stale, underground smell, I came upon a waiting area with long benches against the walls, each occupied by a row of women. Most of them had swollen bellies, some were giving little groans of discomfort. My eye was caught by a wooden sign with the word 'gynaecology' painted on it in red, over a forbiddingly closed door. A few minutes later the door opened a little way to let out an extraordinarily thin woman clutching a prescription. When the next patient stepped into the consulting room, I had just enough time to catch a glimpse of a white-coated figure seated behind a desk before the door closed again.

I was very anxious to get another look at the gynaecologist, to see what sort of man he was, but there was nothing for it but to sit and wait for the next time the door opened. Casting my eye over the women waiting on the benches, I was taken aback by the look of disapproval on their faces. There was no doubt that they were very annoyed.

What they resented, I was quick to realise, was that I was so young, and male to boot. I should have disguised myself as a woman, I thought, I should have stuffed a cushion under my clothes to pretend I was pregnant. The last thing the women in the corridor wanted was to have a teenager in a sheepskin coat in their midst. They sat there looking daggers at me, as if I were a pervert or a Peeping Tom.

What a long wait it was! The door remained firmly shut for what seemed an interminable length of time. It was very hot, and my shirt was drenched with sweat. I was worried that the moisture would make the writing on the inside of my sheepskin coat run, so I decided to take it off.

This prompted the women to exchange agitated whispers. In the half-light of this dank, gloomy corridor they resembled a pack of obese conspirators plotting ways to get rid of me.

'What are you doing here?' snarled one of the women, tapping me on the shoulder.

I turned to look at her. She had short hair and was dressed in trousers and a man's jacket; on her head she wore a green army cap with a red badge showing Mao's head in gold, a clear sign of her outstanding morals. Although she was heavy with child her face was covered in pimples in various stages of eruption or healing. I pitied the child growing in her belly.

I decided to play for time by pretending not to understand. I stared at her stupidly until she was obliged to repeat the question, and then, in slow motion, I cupped my left hand behind my ear in the gesture of the deaf-mute.

'Look, his ear's all bruised and swollen,' said one of the waiting women.

'This is the wrong place for ear diseases!' shouted the woman with the cap, as though convinced of my deafness. 'Ophthalmology is upstairs!'

A heated discussion ensued. And while the women argued about whether I needed an ophthalmologist or an otologist, the door opened. This was the long-awaited opportunity to make a mental note of the gynaecologist's appearance: fortyish, grizzled lanky hair, sharp features, tired-looking, a cigarette dangling from his lips.

After this preliminary reconnaissance I went for a long walk, or rather I strolled up and down the town's single high street. I lost track of how often I walked the distance from the hospital, past the basketball court, to the end of the street and back again. I kept thinking about the doctor. He seemed younger than my father. I could only hope that they had met. I had been told that he was on duty at the gynaecology department on Mondays and Thursdays, and devoted the rest of the week to surgery, urology, and digestive disorders. It was not unlikely that he knew my father, or at any rate had heard of him, as he had been quite famous in the province in the days before he was labelled a class enemy. I tried to picture my father or my mother in the gynaecologist's shoes, finding the Little Seamstress and their beloved son in the consulting room of the district hospital. They would be devastated, it would be the worst thing that could happen to them, worse than the Cultural Revolution! They'd throw us out at once, without giving me a chance to explain that I was not the father. They would refuse to see me ever again. It was insane, but the bourgeois intellectuals upon whom the Communists had inflicted so much hardship were no less strict morally than their persecutors.

That afternoon I went to the restaurant for a meal. Not that I was eager to do so, because the expense was a strain on my tight budget, but it was the only place where you could have an informal chat with strangers. You never knew, I thought, perhaps I'd bump into some shady individual with inside information about procuring abortions.

I ordered a roast chicken with fresh peppers and a bowl of rice. I lingered over my meal – it took me longer than a toothless man to finish, for as the amount of food on my plate dwindled so my confidence ebbed away. Why would any disreputable character risk attracting attention by visiting the restaurant anyway?

For two whole days I made no further progress with my

gynaecological research. The only person with whom I was able to broach the subject was the night watchman of the hospital, a thirty-year-old former policeman who had been dismissed from his post the year before for sleeping with two girls. I stayed with him in his cubicle until midnight, playing chess and exchanging tall stories. He asked me to introduce him to the pretty girls undergoing re-education on the mountain, of whom I claimed to be a connoisseur, but he flatly refused to listen to anything I had to say about my girlfriend having period problems.

'I don't want to know,' he said, clearly alarmed. 'If the hospital management heard of me getting mixed up in that kind of thing they'd accuse me of being a recidivist and send me straight to prison.'

Towards noon on the third day, having lost all hope of gaining access to the gynaecologist, I prepared myself for the return journey up the mountain. Then, quite suddenly, I remembered the old man who used to be a preacher.

I didn't know his name, but remembered seeing him in the audience at the film shows Luo and I attended, with his long silvery hair floating in the breeze. We had liked the look of him. There was an air of nobility about him, even when he was in his blue worker's uniform sweeping the street with a remarkably long-handled broom, even when he was mocked and spat upon by the townsfolk, including five-year-old urchins. For the past twenty years he had been forbidden to practise his faith.

Every time I think of the old preacher I am reminded of the story about how his house was ransacked by the Red Guards. Under his pillow they found a book written in a foreign language that no one could identify. Their reaction was not unlike that of the cripple and his gang when confronted with my copy of *Cousin Pons*. They had to send their booty all the way to the University of Beijing for identification, and it turned out to be a Latin Bible. After his exposure as a member of the Christian faith the unfortunate fellow was forced to spend the rest of his days sweeping Yong Jing's high street from morning to night, rain or shine. By the time Luo and I met him he had become a permanent fixture in the town.

To consult a preacher on the delicate subject of abortion seemed pretty outrageous. Was this business with the Little Seamstress making me lose all sense of proportion, I wondered. Then it occurred to me that I hadn't seen the grizzled street sweeper wielding his long-handled broom with mechanical regularity since I arrived in town three days before.

I asked a cigarette vendor whether the old man had served out his term of forced labour.

'No,' he said. 'He's at death's door, poor soul.'

'What's the matter with him?'

'Cancer. His two sons have come from the city to visit him. They've taken him to hospital.'

Hearing this I turned and broke into a run, although I hardly knew why. I raced up the high street to the other end of town as fast as my legs would carry me. By the time I reached the inpatient department I was completely out of breath, but I knew what I had to do: I would approach the dying preacher-sweeper in a last-ditch appeal for advice.

Once inside the hospital, I was overcome by the confluent smells of disinfectant, overflowing latrines and greasy cooking. The place was like a wartime refugee camp, with the hospital wards doubling as kitchens. There were pans, chopping blocks, kettles, vegetables, eggs, salt cellars, bottles of soy sauce and vinegar scattered every-where: between the patients' beds and among the basins and the metal stands from which the blood transfusion bottles were suspended. At this midday hour most of the patients seemed either to be hunched over some steaming pan, plunging their chopsticks into the broth and squab-bling over the noodles, or busy making omelettes which hissed and sputtered in frying pans full of boiling fat.

The chaos and the noise shocked me. I had no idea that district hospitals were not equipped with proper kitchens and that patients had to see to their own nourishment regardless of how serious their illness was, indeed regard-less of whether they were disabled or even amputees. Covered in red, black or green plasters, with their bandages coming undone and fluttering in the steam rising from the cooking pots, the invalid cooks made a clownish impression.

I found the dying preacher in a ward with six beds. He was on a saline drip. Gathered around him were his two sons and his daughters-in-law, all of them aged about forty. A tearful old woman was preparing food on a small paraffin stove at the foot of his bed. I crouched down beside her.

'Are you his wife?' I asked.

She nodded. Her hands were shaking so badly that I offered to take the eggs and break them over the pan for her.

Both sons wore blue Mao jackets buttoned up to the neck. They had the demeanour of undertakers' assistants or government officials, yet they reminded me of a pair of newshounds in their strenuous efforts to get an old rickety tape recorder to work. The machine was rusty, it rattled and creaked, and the yellow enamel was flaked.

There was a sudden, ear-splitting whine as the recorder came to life, which so alarmed the other patients in the ward that they dropped their bowls, spilling the contents all over their bedclothes.

The younger of the two sons motioned the occupants of the ward to silence, while his brother held a microphone to the preacher's lips.

'Say something Dad, please,' the elder son begged.

The old man's silvery hair had almost all fallen out, and his face had changed beyond recognition. He was a shadow of his former self, with jutting bones and skin like the thinnest sheet of rice paper, yellowed and dull. His body, once robust, had shrunk to half its size. Too weak to move under the tight bedclothes and clearly in pain, he raised his heavy eyelids. This sign of life was noted with surprise and joy by his entourage. The microphone was held to his lips once more, and the recorder started turning with a crunching sound like boots treading on broken glass.

'Dad, please make an effort,' the preacher's son pleaded. 'We want to record your voice for the last time, so that your grandchildren will have something to remember you by.'

'If you could just repeat one of Chairman Mao's sayings – that would be perfect. Just a few words, or a slogan, go on, try! They'll know their grandfather wasn't a reactionary after all, that he'd put all that behind him!'

A slight tremor passed through the preacher's lips as he shaped some words, but there was virtually no sound. For the next minute he struggled on, without anyone catching the gist of his whisperings. Even the old woman had to admit that she could not make head or tail of what he was saying.

Then he lapsed into a coma.

The son rewound the tape, after which the whole family listened again to the mysterious message.

'It's Latin,' the elder son declared. 'He's said his final prayer in Latin.'

'Just like him,' said the old woman, taking out a handkerchief to mop the perspiration on the preacher's forehead.

At that instant I jumped to my feet and made for the door, without a word of explanation. By chance I had caught a glimpse of the white-coated gynaecologist standing ghost-like in the doorway; as if in slow motion, I had seen him take a last drag on his cigarette, exhale the smoke, flick the butt away, and vanish.

In my rush to cross the room I knocked over a bottle of soy sauce and tripped over an empty saucepan someone had left on the floor, which slowed me down. By the time I reached the door there was no sign of the doctor.

I hurried down the corridor in the hope of catching up with him, glancing into each doorway and asking every-one who crossed my path if they knew where he was. In the end a patient pointed his finger to a door all the way at the end.

'I saw him go in there, into the emergency ward. It seems there's been an accident at the Red Flag Factory: someone's hand got caught in a machine and all five of his fingers were cut off.'

When I was in front of the door, which was shut, I could hear the injured man moaning. I gave the door a little push and it gave way at once, without any noise.

Bandages were being applied to the patient, who was sitting up on the hospital bed, naked to the waist, stiff-necked, his head thrown back against the wall. He was about thirty years old, with a tanned, muscular torso and powerful shoulders. I slipped into the room and shut the door behind me. His mutilated hand was dressed with a first layer of gauze. The blood seeped through the white dressing, making stains that spread and dripped into a metal basin on the floor next to the bed, tick-tocking like a broken clock amid the poor man's cries of pain.

The doctor had the same drained look of an insomniac as the first time I spotted him in the consulting room, but he seemed less indifferent now, less remote. He went on unwinding a large roll of gauze and wrapping it round and round the man's hand, without paying attention to me. He was certainly too engrossed in his work to notice my sheepskin coat.

I felt in my pocket for a cigarette, which I lit. Then I stepped up to the bed and, with an almost desultory air, I placed the cigarette in the doctor's mouth, or rather, between his lips, by way of an offering on behalf of the Little Seamstress. Wordlessly he shot me a quick glance, and proceeded to smoke while he occupied himself with the bandages. I lit another cigarette, which I offered to the patient. He took it with the fingers of his right hand.

'Would you help me with this,' the doctor said, passing me one end of the strip of gauze. 'Hold it tight.'

From either side of the bed we pulled the bandage taut, like two men tying a parcel with string.

The flow of blood was staunched, and as the patient's groans subsided the cigarette slipped from his fingers; he promptly fell asleep – the effect of the anaesthetic, the doctor explained.

'Who are you, anyway?' he asked, securing the bandage with a final knot.

'I'm the son of one of the doctors at the provincial

hospital,' I told him. 'Actually, he doesn't work there any more.'

'What's his name?'

It had been my intention to give the name of Luo's father, but my own father's name came out of my mouth. An uncomfortable silence ensued. I had the impression that he had not only heard of my father but also knew about his political troubles.

'What is it you want?' he asked.

'It's my sister. She's been having problems with her periods . . . for close on three months now.'

'Impossible,' he said coldly.

'Pardon?'

'Your father has no daughters. You're a liar – get out of my sight!'

He didn't raise his voice as he said this, nor did he send me away with a dismissive gesture, but I could tell he was very angry. He almost flung his cigarette butt in my face.

Blushing with mortification I headed for the door, but after a few steps I turned to face him and heard myself saying: 'I have a proposition to make: if you can help my girlfriend she'll be grateful to you for the rest of her life, and I'll give you a book by Balzac.'

It was a shock to hear the French author's name being spoken aloud in this clinical environment, this district hospital in the middle of nowhere. The doctor hesitated briefly, then opened his mouth to speak.

'I've already said you are a liar. How could you have got hold of a book by Balzac?'

Without replying, I took off my sheepskin jacket, turned it inside out and showed him the writing on the leather; the ink had faded somewhat, but my script was still legible.

He cast an expert eye over the text, then drew out a packet of cigarettes, offered me one, and lit another for himself, which he smoked as he set about reading in earnest.

'The translation is obviously by Fu Lei,' he murmured. 'I can tell from the style. He's suffered the same fate as your father, poor man: he's been labelled a class enemy.'

His remark brought tears to my eyes. I tried desperately not to cry, but could not help myself, and there I was, snivelling like a kid. It was not the Little Seamstress's predicament that was making me weep, I think, nor was it relief at having come this far in my efforts to save her. It was hearing the name of Fu Lei, Balzac's translator – someone I had never even met. It is hard to imagine a more moving tribute to the gift bestowed by an intellectual on mankind.

This flood of emotion surprised me greatly at the time, and even today I remember it almost more clearly than the events that resulted from my encounter with the doctor. The following Thursday – it was the resourceful physician and lover of literature who set the date – the Little Seamstress, disguised as a thirty-year-old woman with a white band round her forehead, presented herself at the operating theatre. As the perpetrator of the pregnancy had not yet returned from the city, it was I who sat and waited in the corridor for three hours, straining my ears to hear what was going on behind the closed door: distant, muffled sounds, water gushing from a tap, the heart-piercing cry of a woman, soft unintelligible exchanges between nurses, hurried footsteps . . .

The medical intervention was a success. When I was called at last I was taken to a ward reeking of carbolic, where I found the gynaecologist waiting for me. Meanwhile the Little Seamstress was perched on a hospital bed at the far end, putting her clothes on with the help of a nurse.

'It was a girl, if you're interested,' the doctor whispered. He struck a match and lit a cigarette.

The deal we had made was that I would give him our copy of *Ursule Mirouët*, but upon reflection I decided to extend his reward to include the book I treasured most of all – *Jean-Christophe*, which had been translated by the same Fu Lei.

Although she still felt groggy from her ordeal, the Little Seamstress's relief was evident. Indeed, it could not have been greater if she had been facing life imprisonment and had just been found not guilty.

She insisted that there was no need for her to rest at the inn before we set out for home. Instead, she wanted us to visit the cemetery, where the old preacher had been buried two days earlier. She said it was not only thanks to him that I had gone back to the hospital, but that he had also, in some mysterious way, arranged my encounter with the gynaecologist. We spent what little money we had left on a kilo of tangerines to place as an offering on the preacher's grave, which was marked with an inconspicuous slab of cement. We were sorry we didn't know any Latin, and that we were unable to deliver a funerary oration in the language he had employed on his deathbed (either to recite a prayer to his god or to execrate his life as a street sweeper, it was impossible to say which). For a while we debated whether we should take a solemn oath to learn Latin so that we might return one day to address him in that language, and at long last we decided against it, for where would we ever find a Latin primer? (The only place we could think of was Four-Eyes's parental home.) Besides, we would never find anyone to teach us, as we had never heard of there being any other Chinese in these parts who knew Latin.

The inscription on his gravestone was very plain: his name and two dates, that was all. The only indication of the religious office he had once held was a cross in vulgar red paint, as if he had been a pharmacist or a doctor.

We did make one vow, though – that one day, in an imagined future when religions would no longer be prohibited and we ourselves would have plenty of money, we'd come back to erect a handsome, colourful monument to his memory, complete with a carved portrait of a man with silver hair and a crown of thorns like the one Jesus wore. But he wouldn't have nails in the palms of his hands – he'd be holding a long-handled broom.

After this the Little Seamstress said she wanted to visit the old Buddhist temple to throw a few notes over the fence, in gratitude for the mercy shown by the heavenly powers. But the building was boarded up and locked, and we had already spent the last of our money.

THAT'S THE story. Now for the ending. There is just time for you to hear the sound of six matches being struck on a winter's night.

It was three months since the Little Seamstress had had the abortion. The night was dark, and the soft murmur of the wind mingled with the grunts coming from the pigsty. It was also three months since Luo had returned to the mountain.

There was frost in the air. The dry, rasping crack of a striking match broke the silence. The black shadow of our house on stilts looming a few paces away was weakened in the yellow glow and shivered against the backdrop of night.

The match spluttered, was almost snuffed out in its own black smoke, then flared up again as it approached *Père Goriot*. The book was lying on the ground with the others, in front of our house. The flame licked the pages, making them twist and stick together while the words disappeared into the wind. The poor somnambulant French girl was roused by the conflagration, she tried to flee, but it was too late: before she could be reunited with her beloved cousin she too was engulfed in the flames, along with the money-grubbers, her suitors, and the legacy of millions – all went up in smoke.

The next three matches made a funeral pyre of *Cousin Pons*, *Colonel Chabert* and *Eugénie Grandet* respectively. Then it was time for *The Hunchback of Notre Dame*, with Quasimodo hobbling across the flagstones with Esmeralda on his back. The sixth match dealt with *Madame Bovary*. But the flame refused to set fire to the page where Emma lies in bed with her lover in the hotel at Rouen, smoking a cigarette and murmuring 'you'll leave me . . .'. This final match was more selective in its fury, choosing to attack the end of the book, where Emma, in the agony of death, fancies she hears a blind man singing:

> *The heat of the sun of a summer day*
> *Warms a young girl in an amorous way.*

A violin struck up a mournful tune, and at the same instant a sudden gust of wind assailed the bonfire of books, scattering Emma's fresh ashes and mingling them with those of her carbonised compatriots as they were wafted up into the air.

A dusting of ashes clung to the bow as it slid across the gleaming metal strings in which the firelight was reflected. The instrument was mine, and I was the player.

Luo the arsonist, the son of the famous dentist, the romantic lover who had crawled to his beloved on all fours, the admirer of Balzac – Luo was drunk. He sat hunched over the fire, mesmerised by the flames consuming all the stories and characters we had grown to love so dearly. He was crying and laughing by turns.

There were no witnesses to the scene. The villagers,

accustomed to the sound of my violin, no doubt preferred to stay in their warm beds. We would have loved to have our old friend, the miller, with us to play his three-stringed instrument and sing his bawdy old songs while he made the crinkled folds of his stomach roll and ripple. But he was sick: two days earlier, when we visited him, he had come down with the flu.

The auto-da-fé continued. The famous Count of Monte Cristo, who had escaped from the dungeon of a castle on an island in the sea, was likewise fed to the flames of Luo's madness. Nor was there reprieve for any of the other characters, male and female alike, who once inhabited Four-Eyes's suitcase.

Not even the sudden appearance of the village headman would have made us pause in our frenzy. In fact, we were so drunk that we might well have taken him for a character in a novel and burnt him alive.

As it was, the place was deserted. The Little Seamstress had gone, never to return. Her departure, as dramatic as it was sudden, had taken us completely by surprise.

We spent a long time searching our traumatised memories for any hints she may have given of the calamity that was to befall us. In the end we came up with several tell-tale signs, which were for the most part connected with her wardrobe.

About two months earlier Luo had told me she had made herself a brassiere. She had been inspired by something in *Madame Bovary*, he said, whereupon I commented that it would be the first item of lingerie on Phoenix mountain worthy of recording in the local annals.

'Her latest obsession,' Luo continued, 'is to be like a city girl. Next time you hear her talk you'll find she's adopted our accent.'

We attributed her enthusiasm for the brassiere to innocent girlish vanity, but there were two other novelties which, inexplicably, didn't strike us as odd, even though neither of them was suited to mountain wear. To begin with, she had taken back the blue Mao jacket she had made for me with its trio of gilt buttons on each sleeve; the only time I had worn it was when Luo and me paid our official visit to the miller. She had taken the seams in and shortened it to make it look more like a woman's garment, but had kept the four pockets and little stand-up collar. The result was very smart, but in those days such a jacket would only be worn by a woman in the city. Next she had asked her father to buy her a pair of white tennis shoes at the store in Yong Jing. They were as white as chalk, a colour that would not last more than three days on the perpetually muddy paths of the mountain.

I also remember how she looked on the day that marked the Western new year. It wasn't a proper celebration, just a national holiday. Luo and I had gone to see her, as usual. I scarcely recognised her when I stepped into the house: I could have sworn she was a high school student from the city. The long pigtail tied with red ribbon had made way for a short bob, which was very becoming and modern-looking. She was busy putting the final touches to the Mao jacket. Luo was delighted with her transformation, although he was as surprised as I was. He was even more thrilled when the dashing new garment was ready and she slipped it on. In combination with her new hairstyle and her immaculate tennis shoes, the nifty jacket with its mannish details made her look unfamiliarly stylish and sensual. The lovely, unsophisticated mountain girl had vanished without a trace. Studying her new look,

Luo was filled with the happiness of an artist contemplating his finished creation.

'All that time we spent reading to her has certainly paid off,' he whispered in my ear.

That the ultimate pay-off of this metamorphosis, this feat of Balzacian re-education, was yet to come did not occur to us. Were we too wrapped up in ourselves to notice the warning signals? Did we overestimate the power of love? Or, quite simply, had we ourselves failed to grasp the essence of the novels we had read to her?

One morning in February – it was the day before our insane auto-da-fé – Luo and I were at work in a paddy field, each with our own buffalo, when we heard shouts coming from the village. We hurried back to see what the commotion was about, and found the old tailor waiting for us at the house on stilts.

We could tell something was wrong, for he had come unannounced and without his sewing machine, but when we went up to him his gaunt, ravaged face and rumpled hair struck fear into our hearts.

'My daughter left this morning, at first light,' he announced.

'Left?' Luo gasped. 'I don't understand.'

'Nor do I, but that's what she's done.'

He told us that his daughter had applied to the commune leader behind his back to obtain the necessary forms and documents to undertake a long journey. Not until the previous evening had she told him of her plans to change her life and try her chances in the city.

'I asked her if the two of you knew,' he went on. 'She said she hadn't told you, and that she'd write to you as soon as she got settled somewhere.'

'Why didn't you stop her,' Luo lamented, in a barely audible voice.

'Too late, too late,' the old man replied dully. 'I even told her: if you leave now – don't ever come back.'

At this Luo broke away and started running, faster and faster, in a desperate headlong flight down the steep mountain path in pursuit of the Little Seamstress. I went after him, taking a short cut across the rocks. The scene was like one of the bad dreams that had been troubling me lately, with the Little Seamstress losing her footing and falling into the void, and with Luo and me chasing after her, slithering down perpendicular cliffs without a thought of the risk to ourselves. For a moment I lost track of whether I was running in my dream or in reality, or whether I was dreaming as I ran. The rocks were nearly all the same shade of grey, with patches of moist, slippery moss.

Little by little I was outdistanced by Luo. As I ran, taking flying leaps from one boulder to the next and scrambling over rocky outcrops, the ending of my dream came back to me in sharp detail. The ominous cries of the red-beaked raven circling invisibly overhead rang in my ears; any moment now I would spot the body of the Little Seamstress lying at the foot of a cliff, folded double on a bed of rock, with two bleeding gashes reaching from the back of her skull all the way to her finely turned forehead. My muscles ached and my mind reeled. I wondered what was making me chase after Luo across this treacherous mountain slope? Was it friendship? Was it my affection for his girlfriend? Or was I merely an onlooker anxious not to miss the ending of a drama? I couldn't decide which, but still the memory of the old dream kept going round and round in my head.

After two or three hours of running, jumping, slithering, falling, and even somersaulting, in the course of which one of my shoes split open, I finally spotted the Little Seamstress silhouetted against a rock overlooking the graveyard. Seeing her alive and well was an immense relief, and I was able to banish the nightmarish phantoms from my mind.

I slowed my pace until I collapsed in a heap by the footpath, dizzy, exhausted, my stomach heaving.

The setting was familiar. It was there that, a few months previously, I had met the poetess who turned out to be Four-Eyes's mother. How fortunate it was, I told myself, that the Little Seamstress should have chosen to stop here in order to bid her maternal ancestors goodbye, for I couldn't have gone on running for much longer without having a heart attack or losing my mind.

From where I was on the path I had an unobstructed view of their reunion, which started when she turned her head towards the approaching Luo. Just like me, he fell to the ground from exhaustion.

I rubbed my eyes in disbelief as the scene froze into a still image: the girl with the mannish jacket, bobbed hair and white shoes, sitting perfectly still on the rock while the boy lay sprawled on the ground, gazing at the clouds overhead. They didn't seem to be speaking, at least I couldn't hear anything. I almost wished there would be a passionate confrontation, with shouted accusations, explanations, floods of tears, insults, but there was only silence. But for the cigarette smoke curling up from Luo's mouth, you would have taken them for stone statues.

Under the circumstances an outpouring of rage and cold silence amounted to much the same thing, and anyway it would be hard to compare the merits of two so radically different styles of apportioning blame, yet it occurred to me that Luo might be mistaken in his strategy, or at any rate too quick to resign himself to the pointlessness of argument.

I gathered some branches and dead leaves to make a fire under the overhanging rock. I reached into the little bag I had brought with me and drew out a few sweet potatoes, which I buried in the embers.

Secretly, and for the first time ever, I was angry with the Little Seamstress. Although I was fully aware of my role as spectator, I felt just as betrayed as Luo, not by her decision to leave the mountain, but by the fact that she had not thought to tell me about it. I felt as if all the complicity we had shared in procuring the abortion had been wiped from her consciousness, as if I had never meant more to her than a friend of a friend, which was what I would remain for ever.

With a pointed stick I speared a sweet potato from among the smoking embers, tapped it against a rock, blew away the dirt and ashes. Then suddenly I heard voices: the two statues were talking. Although they spoke softly, they were clearly agitated. I caught the name of Balzac, and wondered what any of this could possibly have to do with him.

I was glad the silence had been broken, but before I had time to adjust my hearing to their conversation the stone figures leaped into motion: Luo scrambled to his feet and she jumped down from her rock. But instead of throwing herself into her despairing lover's arms, she grabbed her bundle and strode off down the path.

'Wait,' I shouted, waving the sweet potato. 'Come and have some of these! I made them especially for you!'

At my first shout she hastened her step, at my second

she broke into a run, and at my third she took off like a bird, growing smaller and smaller until she vanished.

Luo came to sit with me by the fire. He was very pale. Not a word of complaint or grief crossed his lips. It was a few hours before the auto-da-fé.

'She's gone,' I said.

'She wants to go to the city,' he said. 'She mentioned Balzac.'

'What about him?'

'She said she had learnt one thing from Balzac: that a woman's beauty is a treasure beyond price.'